"I told the agency I wanted an older woman."

His voice had a throaty edge to it. He shook his head and his displeasure seemed to deepen. "You are not at all what I expected—or wanted."

Already ill-at-ease, Diana thought him unnecessarily abrupt. "I should have thought you'd be glad to get anyone!" she retorted, and she saw his eyes narrow.

"Impertinent! Young and impertinent!" he growled. "And what makes you think I should be so undiscriminating."

"Your manservant implied you had difficulty hiring anyone, or getting them to stay."

Giacomo Ortoni's face darkened still further. "Your name?"

The rapped-out question startled Diana. There was no way she could give her real name....

Annabel Murray has pursued many hobbies. She helped found an arts group in Liverpool, England, where she lives with her husband and two daughters. She loves drama: she appeared in many stage productions and went on to write an award-winning historical play. She uses all her experiences—holidays being no exception—to flesh out her characters' backgrounds and create believable settings for her romance novels.

Books by Annabel Murray

THE EAGLE OF SOLAMENZA

Annabel Murray

Harlequin Books

TORONTO • NEW YORK • LONDON
AMSTERDAM • PARIS • SYDNEY • HAMBURG
STOCKHOLM • ATHENS • TOKYO • MILAN

Original hardcover edition published in 1989
by Mills & Boon Limited

ISBN 0-373-17067-X

Harlequin Romance first edition August 1990

For all my friends at Southport Writers' Circle
for their unfailing support and
constructive criticism

CHAPTER ONE

'WHAT on earth's eating *you*, Di? Why the long face? You've always been potty about Rome. I thought you were looking forward to this trip?'

'Aye, I was, but I'm not now.' The soft Scottish voice was doleful.

Labelled by a former boyfriend as 'a small bundle of fun and energy', Diana McWinter was petite and blonde with an outgoing, bubbly personality. Her happy disposition meant that she was rarely seen wearing a gloomy expression. Hence her friend and fellow courier's surprise.

'Why ever not?' Susan demanded to know. 'It's not Friday the thirteenth!' Susan knew of and was amused by her friend's superstitious nature. 'And I see you're wearing your lucky cat. So why?'

'Because of Julia!'

'Julia? I've never heard you mention anyone of that name.'

Diana's startlingly blue eyes were rueful.

'No, you haven't! And you'll understand why, when I *do* tell you about her. But let's wait till we've got this lot sorted out and on to the plane, then I'll explain.'

The two girls—both well-versed tour guides—were waiting, with their charges, in the departure lounge of Heathrow airport for the Air Italia flight to Rome.

Having been born and lived in a small Scottish town for most of her life, Diana had always wanted a career that involved travel. And after leaving school with two good A-levels, both in languages, she had taken a polytechnic course in tourism.

The recently assembled travellers were eyeing each other warily. It would be a while, Diana knew from experience, before conversations were struck up and holiday friendships made. So, putting her personal feelings aside, she went into action, answering questions—however fatuous, reassuring nervous first-timers, checking on any special requirements.

A tour party such as this could be fraught with problems. Many of the travellers were elderly, and the two girls needed to know what, if any, medication they were taking. They had to be prepared to deal with broken limbs, heart attacks and similar emergencies. Above all, it was their task to keep their charges happy.

But at last their flight number was called, and with the passengers, for the moment at least, handed over into the care of the air hostesses and the aircraft ready for take-off, Diana and Susan had time to breathe.

'Right!' said Susan as Diana sank thankfully into the seat beside her. 'Now you can tell me what's up. And who's this Julia?'

'You've heard me talk of my Aunt Marion and Uncle Alastair in Edinburgh? Well, Julia is—or perhaps I should say was, I'm not sure which—you'll see why in a minute—Aunt Marion and Uncle Alastair's adopted daughter.'

'That's the Uncle Alastair that just died? Your father's brother?'

'Aye.' Diana adjusted her seat-belt. 'And what's up is that I shan't be able to go on to Florence after all.'

Diana was due for a holiday. At the end of the coming fortnight she had planned to leave the tourists in Susan's capable hands for the flight home and stay on in Italy for another two weeks. She'd been to Florence once or twice in charge of tourist groups, but she longed to have some time there just to herself, and somehow she had never managed to achieve this ambition.

'But why can't you go to Florence?' Susan asked as the aircraft lifted off the ground. 'Has His Nibs cancelled your holiday?' This disrespectful term was the girls' private name for their boss.

'No. It's all because of Julia. I've never told you about my dreadful cousin.'

'No, you haven't!' Susan said somewhat indignantly. During the three years they'd worked together the two girls had become good friends and generally confided in each other. 'She's adopted, you said?'

'Aye. Auntie Marion and Uncle Alastair couldn't have bairns of their own. Well, it's Julia's fault—even though indirectly—that I've had to change my plans. It seems Julia's disappeared. And I've got to try and find the wretched girl. Thank you,' Diana accepted a tray from one of the air hostesses who was already serving lunch.

'You certainly don't sound very sorry about Julia's disappearance,' Susan remarked shrewdly when the hostess had moved on.

Diana's pert little features contracted into a grimace and she stabbed her fork into a slice of tomato as if the offending morsel were Julia, her *bête noire*.

'If I were ever to adopt a bairn and it turned out like Julia I think I'd be *glad* if she disappeared.'

'But obviously your aunt doesn't feel that way?'

'No. Poor old Marion's never been able to see how selfish and ungrateful Julia is, and now that Uncle Alastair's dead she's determined to find her. Personally I'm not convinced she really *is* missing.'

'Well, supposing she is, how long is it since your aunt heard from her?'

'About a year. Two years ago Julia and a couple of girlfriends set off to travel round Europe. They were gone for a month. Then the other two came home, without her.'

'If she's as awful as you say I suppose they fell out?'

'Maybe. I don't know about that. They *said* Julia had met a man—an Italian—and had decided to stay in Italy. Of course Auntie Marion was frantic. She was all for setting off there and then to bring Julia home. But, as Uncle Alastair pointed out, Julia wasn't a bairn any more, she was nineteen. Besides, they didn't really know where to start looking for her.'

'Didn't her two friends know?'

'Not really. All they could tell Marion and Alastair was that the man's name was Ortoni, that he was devastatingly attractive, a lot older than Julia and that he seemed to be enormously rich.'

'And didn't Julia get in touch with her parents herself?'

'Oh, aye—eventually.' Diana pushed her empty plate aside and started on the trifle which constituted the sweet course. 'Though, knowing Julia, I'm surprised she even bothered. But Marion finally did get a letter. It wasn't very long and it didn't tell them much except that Julia was going to marry this man and that she would be the Countess Ortoni, if you please!'

'A countess?' Susan was visibly impressed.

'Aye, and to me that explained a lot of things. Julia was always a raving snob. From the moment she discovered she was adopted she was convinced that she had "blue blood". She was determined to find out who her real parents were, and the moment she was old enough she did.'

'And?'

Diana chuckled, an attractively husky sound.

'Much to her disgust—and my delight—I have to admit it, though it sounds catty—they turned out to be perfectly ordinary people. Not that I ever heard very much about them. Even if I'd felt like questioning Julia, I doubt if she'd have told me. And when I asked Mum she just shook her head and pursed up her lips—like this.' Diana's shapely red lips screwed up into a disapproving prune. 'So I've always had the idea there was some kind of skeleton in the cupboard. Anyway, from then on Julia was bent on redressing the balance. She always had loads of boyfriends. But none of them was ever good enough for her.'

'So an Italian count must have seemed like the answer to a maiden's prayer,' Susan suggested. 'And did she go on writing to her parents?'

'Very rarely. For the first year she sent the occasional postcard, never with any address on it. Knowing Julia I'd say she spun this count some yarn about her ancestry and didn't want her middle-class background catching up with her. Then, about a year ago, even the postcards stopped.'

'Then if it's been that long, why the sudden anxiety to find her now?'

'Dad and Uncle Alastair might have had middle-class origins,' Diana said wryly, 'but Alastair wasn't poor by any means. When his will was read they discovered he'd left Julia quite a substantial legacy. If she *is* married to a count it's unlikely she needs it, but Marion is insistent that she be found.'

'And you've been lumbered with finding her? But why you?'

'Marion's too frail to travel abroad herself and if it becomes necessary I suppose she'll engage a professional detective. But in the meantime, as I'm going to be 'on the spot', as she calls it, she wants *me* to make some preliminary enquiries. And I suppose she thinks she can trust me to be discreet if there's any scandal.'

'Scandal?' At this hint of an even more fascinating turn to the story, Susan leaned nearer to her friend. 'What kind of scandal?'

'Aunt Marion's never been really easy in her mind about Julia's marriage—even though, as Mum says, it did at least confer respectability on Julia's behaviour.'

'Why?'

'Well, for a start there's no proof the wedding even took place. And then, although Uncle Alastair was well travelled before his marriage, Marion's always been rather insular. She dislikes and distrusts all 'foreigners'. Mentally she's still living in the era of 'white slave traffic'. She's convinced herself—and even more so since the cards stopped coming—that Julia's either been foully murdered or fallen into the hands of some unscrupulous adventurer. That he might not *be* a count.'

There was a break in the story as the air hostess collected their trays, then, 'Where were the cards posted?' asked Susan. 'That might help?'

'Mostly from Rome. Occasionally the postmark was "Solamenza", which none of us had ever heard of. But His Nibs has some detailed maps in his office. I looked it up and it seems Solamenza's in an area of southern Italy known as the Abruzzi.'

'So where do you think you'll start?'

'In Rome, touch wood! I'm hoping I won't have to go to this Solamenza place. Judging by the map it's in pretty remote, rugged country. Surely,' Diana appealed to her friend, 'if this man *is* a count, someone in Rome will have heard of him?'

'Mmm, I should think so. But it's a bit ironic, isn't it, you having to find your cousin, if you've never liked her?'

'Aye. I've always been rather ashamed of disliking her so much. But it's that old saying, isn't it, "you can choose your friends but not your relations"? She's only two years younger than me, and even when we were quite wee she had some very unlikeable traits.'

'Such as?'

'For one thing, she was an awful wee liar. She'd tell any kind of lie to keep out of trouble. And she'd tell lies about other people—me in particular. A real troublemaker. And she had a terrible temper. If things didn't go her way she'd throw herself on the floor, cry and scream and hold her breath. My mum used to say she needed a good smack. But she used to frighten the life out of Marion, so much so that eventually Julia got whatever it was she wanted.'

'Spoiled, obviously,' commented Susan.

'Aye. But I think there was more to it than that. It seems to me there's a lot to be said for genes and heredity. Mum always said it was a bit of a risk adopting a bairn, that you could never tell what might "come out". And I'm sure it can't have been environment in Julia's case. Aside from her prejudices, Marion's a lovely person and Alastair was a nice man too. Perhaps they did spoil Julia a bit, but not to *that* extent.'

'Well, *I* think it's all rather exciting,' Susan, an incurable romantic, said. 'It could turn out to be quite an adventure. I wish I was coming with you.'

'*I* wish you were coming with me,' Diana said emphatically. 'Because I'm not looking forward to it a bit.' Then, with determined brightness, 'but I'm not going to think about it any more for the next two weeks. I'm going to enjoy Rome—I always do—and see that this lot . . .' she jerked her bright blonde head towards their fellow passengers '. . . enjoy it too. *Then* I'll start to think about Julia and her wretched count—if he exists.'

Despite her distaste for her forthcoming task, many-coloured Rome had lost none of its enchantment for Diana. As always she revelled in the brilliance of Raphael and Michelangelo, the splendour of the Papal Guard, the beauty of the doves that fluttered down from the shadows of St Peter's to search for crumbs amid the feet of the passers-by.

Ochre and sienna, russet and red brick, creamy stone and blue-grey domes, the gleam of marble, all were offset by the greens of pine and cyprus.

From the window of her hotel bedroom she had a sweeping view of the city—St Peter's and the Vatican palaces; the cupolas, towers and roofscape of the historic centre spreading out to the southern suburbs.

There were plenty of subjects for photography and the camera-happy members of the little group of tourists thoroughly enjoyed their holiday, returning each day to their hotel with reels of exposed film. Others were content to load themselves with souvenirs—portraits of the Pope, all kinds of religious articles, replicas of the Colosseum and the she-wolf suckling Romulus and Remus. And, happily for the two girls and their party, the fortnight was incident-free.

It was very tempting, after Diana had seen Susan and her charges off at the airport, to spend another few days in self-indulgent enjoyment of the Eternal City.

It was Holy Week. Hundreds of tourist coaches with foreign licence plates clogged the narrow streets of downtown Rome, further complicating the chronic traffic conditions. Holidaymakers and pilgrims were everywhere, picnicking on church steps and leaving their sandwich wrappings and soft-drink cans behind.

Yet not all of Rome was swamped by tourists. There were still many alluring quiet corners, many beautiful things to see. But Diana's always active conscience would not permit the delay in carrying out her aunt's commission.

It seemed sensible to begin her enquiries at the British Consulate in Rome. A very helpful young man there had never heard of a Count Ortoni himself, but promised to ask amongst his colleagues and Roman friends.

'If you leave me your hotel telephone number I'll call you. In the meantime I suggest you carry on enjoying Rome.'

Diana needed no second urging and spent two supremely happy days. But on the evening of the second day she returned to her hotel to find a written message waiting for her.

'I have been unable to discover anything about a *Count* Ortoni,' the note read. 'And in fact there are only three Ortonis listed for the whole of Rome.' There followed three names and addresses. 'I can only suggest you make enquiries of these people. Let me know if you think I can give you any more help.'

For want of a better idea, Diana decided to try the names and addresses in the order in which they were given. The first on the list was an E. Ortoni, the address being in one of the busiest spots in central Rome. The building was an old rather unprepossessing house converted into apartments. It seemed an unlikely spot to find a *soi-disant* count.

As in many residential buildings in the city, the main entrance door was closed. Visitors were required to use the *citofono*, an intercom system, to ask for admittance. Diana pressed the button corresponding with the given apartment number and at once the door opened electrically.

There was no lift, and she mounted the uncarpeted stairs, feeling more and more certain that she was on the wrong track. On the third floor she found the door she was looking for and pressed the doorbell. After a while there were the sounds of someone approaching, and then Diana was aware that she was being looked at through a peephole in the centre panel of the door. It was an uncanny sensation and her hand went to the lucky black cat she wore at her throat.

'*Si?*' a woman's voice enquired.

'I'm looking for someone called Ortoni,' Diana volunteered in Italian. 'A *Count* Ortoni?'

The response to this was a rather coarse laugh and then the door opened to reveal a blowsy-looking redhead of indeterminate age.

'You are English?' the woman said in that tongue. Diana sighed. But she'd given up trying to explain that she came from Scotland and was British rather than English. Also she rather prided herself on her languages and was a little piqued at being so easily discovered. But she nodded. 'I am Elsa Ortoni,' the woman informed her. 'But you will find no count here. Unless he is using an assumed name.'

Other doors around the landing were opening cautiously and curious ears were listening to their conversation. Elsa Ortoni opened her door a little wider.

'But you may come in and see for yourself.'

A little dubiously, Diana stepped inside the apartment and the door closed behind her.

'The man I'm looking for may not really be a count,' she explained. 'Do you have a husband? Or a son?'

Again there came that rather raucous laugh.

'No sons. But many . . . daughters.' As she spoke Elsa Ortoni ushered Diana into a large opulently furnished sitting-room, an astonishing contrast to the rest of the house.

Draped around the plush-upholstered furniture in various conditions of undress were about half a dozen remarkably attractive women who regarded Diana with uninterest. It would have taken far less intelligence than Diana possessed to guess what this place was. Prostitution, she knew, had flourished in Rome since time immemorial.

Elsa Ortoni was quick-witted too and she saw the realisation dawn in Diana's blue eyes.

'You see why your "count"—if he visits here—might use an assumed name.'

'Of . . . of course,' said Diana, then, 'I'm sorry to have bothered you.' She turned to leave, but the redheaded woman was barring her passage and again she felt a slight *frisson* of alarm.

'Don't go, English girl,' Elsa Ortoni said. 'This man has deceived you, perhaps? You have a photograph of him? Possibly we may be able to help you. This is no common bordello,' she added with a touch of pride. 'We have a wealthy *protettore*. It is a high-class place, important people come here. One of them may know your count.'

'No . . . it's all right, really. I must go,' Diana said. 'I . . . I have some other addresses to try.' And this time she sidestepped firmly around the older woman and gained the door. She did not breathe easily until she reached the pavement outside.

She was about to cross to the opposite side of the street when the sudden rush of a small motorcycle ridden by two young men made her step back hastily, but too late. A hand reached out and grabbed her bag from beneath her arm.

The same gesture upset her balance and she fell heavily, striking her head hard against the edge of the pavement.

She must have been knocked out, for the next thing she knew was that she was lying on a soft plush surface, that women's voices were exclaiming over her and she had a splitting headache.

Cautiously she opened her eyes. The first thing she saw was Elsa Ortoni's face, filled with concern.

'I was watching from the window and I saw the *scippatori* rob you. It happens many times a day in Rome. The *carabinieri* seem powerless to arrest the culprits. Maria here will bathe your head.' One of the girls was standing at Elsa's side holding a basin and a cloth, and Diana realised the wet sensation on the side of her face was that of trickling blood.

The women were very kind to her, exclaiming over bruises and torn tights. A cup of tea was offered, and if Diana had not protested firmly a lacing of brandy would have been added.

'Have you been robbed of much?' asked Elsa.

'No.' Diana was not unacquainted with the crime rate in Rome. 'Fortunately I don't carry much cash on me, and my passport is in the hotel safe.'

She was still sitting on one of the plush sofas, sipping her tea, far more at her ease with these women than she would have imagined possible ten minutes ago, when a visitor was shown in. Diana was startled and not a little scandalised to see that he wore the garb of a priest.

'Don Ottavio has come to give us the Holy Week blessing,' Elsa explained to Diana as the priest proceeded to sprinkle the assembled women—including Diana—with holy water. And with a grinned aside, 'He hopes some day to save us all from ruin!'

The blessing over, the priest approached Diana, a look of kindly concern on his ascetic face. He sat down beside her.

'And what is your name, my child?'

'Diana McWinter, *Padre*.'

'And where are you from?'

'Scotland, *Padre*.'

'Ah, yes—a beautiful country. But I am disturbed to see you here, my child. I would not like a foreign girl to be led astray by these misguided women.' His English was so halting that this time Diana answered him in his own language.

'I'm only here by chance, *Padre*,' she told him. 'Elsa and her friends have been very good to me. I was robbed in the street outside.'

'Ah, yes,' his expression was wry, 'Elsa and her kind have hearts of gold, which often, alas, leads to their downfall. You know what they are, my child?' She nodded. 'You will not be staying here?' And as Diana shook her head, 'You are a tourist?'

'In a way. I'm also trying to trace a missing relative, my cousin.'

'Then I wish you success.' He rose to his feet. 'You have means? You have not been robbed of your money?' And, 'You will take care into whose company your search takes you?'

'I'll be all right, *Padre*,' she assured him.

'Then I give you my blessing.' He did so. Then, firmly, 'You will leave here now, my child.' It was a gentle instruction, not a command, and Diana nodded her agreement.

When the priest had gone, Diana too took her leave, thanking Elsa for her help. Despite her protests to the contrary she still felt a little shaken by the robbery and her head still throbbed a little. She decided not to pursue her enquiries that day but to return to her hotel.

The second address she had been given—that of an I. Ortoni—turned out to be an apartment near the Piazza Ungheria in the wealthy Parioli district of Rome. A maid answered the door and ushered her into a large drawing-room furnished with antiques and hung with paintings and drawings. Diana, who had always been interested in the history of art, recognised among others a Degas, a Renoir and a Picasso. This was certainly a more likely setting for a Count!

But again it seemed she was to be disappointed. I. Ortoni was another woman, tall, dark-haired and svelte, who came towards her with outstretched hand.

'*Buon giorno.* I am Iolanda Ortoni,' she told Diana. 'How may I help you? Who has recommended me to you?' And as Diana looked a little blank, 'You *are* a client?'

Iolanda Ortoni, it turned out, was a freelance decorator who also dabbled in the art trade. New business came to her principally through word of mouth. She had her own team of painters, paperhangers, cabinet-makers and other craftsmen on call and willing to work for her.

'No, I'm sorry,' Diana told this cool, very self-assured woman. 'I'm not a client.' And she explained her errand. To her surprised relief Iolanda Ortoni did not at once deny any knowledge of a count of the same name. Instead, with her fine eyes slightly narrowed, she asked,

'What do you want with the Count Ortoni?'

'You know him?' Diana asked eagerly.

'Perhaps,' was the cautious reply.

'Oh, please, either you do or you don't. It's very important that I should find him—if he really does exist.'

'You doubt his existence?' For the first time the sophisticated Italian woman seemed surprised out of her poise. 'Then why are you looking for him?'

For a moment Diana hesitated. But then she realised that only by confiding the details of her errand could she expect to receive equal frankness.

'May I sit down?' she asked. 'It's rather a long story.'

'Please!' The other woman indicated a chair.

As Diana talked Iolanda Ortoni's handsome face remained blandly inscrutable, although once or twice she drew in a sharp breath as though she were about to speak. But she heard Diana out to the end of her tale. Then she questioned her closely. At last she seemed satisfied.

'*Si*, I'm sure the man you are looking for *is* Giacomo Ortoni. He is,' the older woman's face twisted with distaste, 'a distant connection of our family. But he does not live in Rome and he does not come here very often.' She hesitated, then, 'My brother Vitto has had . . .' she paused, 'dealings with him.'

'And he *is* a count?' Diana demanded.

The other woman gave a scoffing little laugh.

'*Si*, by descent. But these days noble titles are not used. He is plain *Signor* Ortoni.' She sounded as if this gave her some peculiar satisfaction. 'But he is very rich.' And now the older woman's features assumed an expression which might well be interpreted as envy. But surely Iolanda Ortoni couldn't be hard up, Diana thought, looking around her.

'I was hoping to find Signor Ortoni in Rome,' Diana sighed. 'But I suppose now I shall have to go all the way to Solamenza.'

'Not necessarily. That is the family home, of course, but he is not always there.' The Italian woman's expression became almost a sneer. 'You are more likely to find Giacomo at the Ortoni *palazzo* in Firenze—you would say Florence.'

'Forgive me if I sound impertinent,' Diana said hesitantly, 'but I get the impression that you dislike Signor Ortoni.'

'Dislike!' Iolanda gave a harsh laugh. 'That is an understatement. Our side of the family have always detested his. Vitto and I are the only ones left of our line—and but for Giacomo Ortoni . . .' She broke off at this interesting point and went on, 'Be warned, Signorina McWinter, in your business with Giacomo Ortoni you are dealing with the descendant of unscrupulous, treacherous men. However, if you are still determined to see him,' she rose and moved towards a dainty little escritoire, 'I will give you his address.'

As Diana left Iolanda Ortoni's apartment, the other woman delivered a parting shot.

'If you are in Rome again I should be very interested to learn the outcome of your meeting with Giacomo.' And, 'But have a care, Signorina McWinter. Remember—like his ancestors, he is a dangerous man to cross.'

Florence! The lofty dome of the Cathedral, Giotto's Campanile, the River Arno dividing the townscape into two unequal parts against a backdrop of olive groves and vineyards set on blue hills.

Yet it was not just a relic of the Renaissance, but a Renaissance city that had endured into the twentieth century. The narrow streets, lined by churches with blank unfinished façades, amplified the sounds of traffic.

And at street level the city was very different from the lovely warm views of rust-coloured roofs, towers and domes familiar from travel brochures. Enclosed in its ring of hills, Florence was hot and humid, noisy, smelly, chaotic, bursting with noisy, argumentative Latin vitality. There were strange anomalies. Modern shops and snack bars operated out of buildings that were standing when Henry VIII came to the English throne.

In fact Diana always thought that if the network of television aerials could be blanked out the scene would be just as it was depicted in eighteenth-century prints. Pavements were almost non-existent and motor-scooters buzzed like hornets through its narrow cobbled streets, endangering the surging herds of tourists. And, as always, Diana loved it.

The only problem with Florence was that with so many beautiful artistic treasures to see the tourist was spoiled for choice. But she was not here to tour galleries and churches.

On the morning after her arrival in the city, she left the old-fashioned *pensione* close to the River Arno and, following the directions Iolanda Ortoni had given her, she made her way through a winding labyrinth of back streets lined with narrow-breasted houses whose overhanging eaves nearly met in the middle. Once beyond this medieval area the way opened out into wider streets and squares until finally, in a quiet street of shuttered *palazzi*, she came to large, locked iron gates that guarded the Florentine residence of Giacomo Ortoni.

A tall building, with its stern-faced, creeper-clad façade and columned courtyard, it was obviously one of the old private palaces with which Florence had once abounded. Sadly, these days many of them had been converted into hotels. Diana took a deep breath and pressed a bell set in the ornate ironwork.

The severe aspect of the *palazzo* was reinforced by the

warder-like appearance of the man who answered the bell's summons. A tall, heavily built hulk with unprepossessing features, he regarded Diana with suspicion and their conversation was conducted in Italian.

'Signor Ortoni?' Diana asked.

'You have an appointment with the Conte?' He stressed the title. So whatever Iolanda Ortoni might say or think, her distant relative insisted on its observance.

'No,' Diana confessed, 'I just called on the off-chance.'

'These agencies,' the man grumbled as he began to wrestle with the recalcitrant fastenings of the gate. 'They are run by idle, inefficient . . .'

'Agencies?' Diana enquired as she entered the courtyard.

'I understood from the Conte that they had no one suitable at present.' The man continued his discontented monologue. 'And then to send someone without an appointment!'

The quick-witted Diana was beginning to see how this information might work to her advantage. On the journey to Florence she had begun to wonder about the wisdom of laying all her cards upon the table before Giacomo Ortoni. Although she was accustomed to making up her own mind about the character of anyone she met—and she had not altogether liked Iolanda Ortoni—she could not help but be influenced by her talk with the other woman. Her implications regarding her relative had made him sound a rather sinister individual, just what Diana's Aunt Marion suspected.

However, if he could be persuaded to employ her . . . She brushed aside the fact that she had only two weeks at her disposal. For surely that would be long enough for her purpose? She could always plead dissatisfaction with her situation and leave.

'Then the . . . the position hasn't been filled?' she asked, hoping that by delicate probing she might be able to discover just what kind of employee Giacomo Ortoni was seeking. But there was no need for finesse.

'No, and once you have met the little *signorina* you will not stay long. No one does.' The man preceded her into a vast, classical entrance hall. And why the Conte wishes her to learn English is beyond me. One would have thought he'd had enough of the English and their ways!'

Diana felt that things were progressing far better than she had had any right to expect. But who on earth was the 'little *signorina*' referred to? Julia had not been married long enough to have a daughter old enough to be learning English. She decided not to risk any further questions. She felt she knew enough to let matters take their own course.

Like many buildings of its age most of the architectural emphasis of the Ortoni *palazzo* had been given to the first floor, or *piano nobile*. And Diana followed her still-complaining guide up a flight of stairs and into a graciously proportioned *salone*. Here she was commanded to wait.

The room was furnished with costly period treasures. Diana knew very little about such things, but looking at the glass-fronted cabinets with their collections of glass and china, even she knew the contents must be priceless.

But it was the portraits ranked all along one wall of the *salone* that really held her gaze. Giacomo Ortoni's ancestors? Yes, and but for the variations in costume they could all have been representations of the same man.

In each portrait, arresting green eyes on either side of a haughty aquiline nose looked out of aristocratic features. And in each case Diana felt as though the eyes held hers in a long enigmatic, compelling stare.

Beneath each painting a brass plate gave a name and a

date. Every so often the same name recurred. There were Tancreds, Humberts, Rainulfs and Giacomos. So the present generation had not broken with tradition.

The distant sound of voices raised as though in anger drew her from her study of the painted Ortonis. Curious to see the disputants, she tiptoed from the *salone* and leaned over the balcony, peering down into the hall whose slender fluted columns rose two storeys to support the domed ceiling above her.

Two men stood in the centre of the mosaic-tiled area. One was the brutish-looking character who had admitted her. The other was taller, of slighter build, and even as she watched he turned and made for the stairs.

Unprepared for his sudden movement, Diana was not swift enough to withdraw, and the man mounting the stairs raised his head and saw her.

She could not prevent a little indrawn hiss of breath. And as always in moments of crisis her hand went to her throat in that little automatic gesture to touch the lucky charm. This man was all that the portraits personified—and more.

He was taller than most Italians, and the subtly striped wool suit he wore did not detract from his aura of toughness. She found him very handsome with his clear golden skin and perfectly turned features. Thick jet-black hair waved back from an intelligent brow, and as he came closer, subjecting her to a keen appraisal, she saw the eyes, familiar to her from the portraits, were a deep, intense green, fringed with thick black lashes.

As he strode towards her, Diana was aware of an overpowering, red-blooded virility. The energy that flowed from him was like a magnetic force.

She was aware too of being rapidly assessed from head to toe. The green eyes noted every detail of her small but softly rounded body, emphasised by her white cotton jeans and the T-shirt that clung to her breasts, unconfined because of the heat by any bra.

'*Signorina*?' His throaty voice had an edge to it. 'Tomaso tells me you are from the *au pair* agency in Rome.' His English was good, almost without accent. 'But I told them I wanted an older woman.' He came closer and she caught the enticing warmth of his body, exuding the spicy male fragrance of his after-shave. 'No!' He shook his dark head and his displeasure seemed to deepen. 'You are not at all what I expected—or wanted.'

Already on edge, Diana thought him unnecessarily abrupt.

'I should have thought you'd be glad to get *anyone*!' she retorted. Her usually soft Scottish lilt had an edge to it and she saw his eyes narrow.

His lower lip was full, hinting at passion, but the upper one was narrow, speaking of impatience, of a quick temper, and now temper predominated.

'Impertinent! Young *and* impertinent!' he growled. 'And what makes you think I should be so undiscriminating?'

'Your manservant implied that you had difficulty getting anyone, or getting them to stay.'

Giacomo Ortoni's face darkened further.

'I must speak to Tomaso. I do not encourage those who work for me to discuss my affairs. Your name?' The sudden change of subject, the rapped-out question, startled Diana, and again she fiddled nervously with the black-cat charm at her neck. However, she was not going to let this Italian browbeat her, and she met his startling green eyes levelly enough even though she was about to lie to him. For there was no way she could give him her real name—the same surname as Julia's.

'Diana Watt,' she told him.

'Diana!' He turned the name over on his tongue. 'Hmm,' he shook his dark, handsome head, 'once I would have thought it an appropriate name for an Englishwoman—Diana the relentless huntress, cold and unyielding. But now I know differently. Some of them can be relentless, it is true. But cold? No, I think not.' And, as Diana was beginning to feel embarrassed, 'Well, Signorina Watt, tell me why I should employ you. Your countrywomen have had a significant lack of success in my household. What makes you think you would be any different from the rest?'

Again she refused to be intimidated by the bright probe of his eyes. Chin elevated, she answered his question.

'I don't give up easily—on anything.'

Surprisingly he nodded agreement.

'Si—relentless, as I said. And tell me, what is your attitude—towards men? Are you chaste?'

'I don't think that's any of your business!' she told him indignantly.

'Oh, but it is, signorina. You see, if I offer you this position—and I am by no means decided on that—you will be, for the most part, working in a household composed entirely of men.'

Diana had a wicked sense of humour which in her schooldays had frequently got her into scrapes. These days she took care to restrain that humour, but even so, 'Och, if they're all like the one who answered the door,' she retorted, 'you needn't worry.'

She saw a reluctant flicker of amusement in his eyes.

'Tomaso may be ugly,' he agreed, 'but, appearances to the contrary, he is human.'

Diana's work, her travels, had brought her into contact

with many men, quite a few of whom had shown her unwanted attentions. But she had never found it an insuperable problem.

'I'll cope,' she told Giacomo Ortoni.

Throughout this exchange both had remained standing, but now he indicated a chair. As Diana obeyed the gesture he seated himself opposite, throwing one long leg across the other in a negligent manner, revealing socks that were an impeccable match for his suit. The action also tightened the soft trouser material across his thighs, and again Diana knew that heightened awareness of his masculinity.

'Why do you wish to work for me, Signorina Watt?'

Again, with a smile, she attempted to lighten the exchange.

'I didn't want to work for you in particular. I just wanted a job in Italy.'

This time he allowed his mouth to relax into a half-smile.

'Then if *I* am not the one so honoured, *signorina*, why Italy?'

'I like Italy.' About this much at least she could be truthful. 'I want to get to know it better—and improve my Italian, of course,' she added as an afterthought, thankful that their conversation had been in English. She particularly did not want Giacomo Ortoni to know just how fluent she was in his language.

'I see!' He shifted in his chair, re-crossing his legs. But this time Diana kept her eyes studiously on his face, though goodness knew that was a devastating enough experience. She had never been particularly attracted to Italian men, but there was something very compelling about this one. In the possibly suspicious circumstances of Julia's disappearance she certainly hadn't expected to feel any such sensations towards Julia's—presumed—husband.

'Tell me more about yourself,' he invited. And as she began to reel off a list of her educational qualifications, 'No, no—about *yourself*—your likes, your dislikes, your family background. It is your character that interests me.'

It was such a novel approach to an interview that Diana just stared at his handsome face for a moment or two, her blue, widely-spaced eyes proclaiming her mystification. But then she gathered her wits.

'I'm twenty-three . . .'

'Twenty-three?' he interrupted. 'You look much younger. I would have thought nineteen at the most. But twenty-three and still only an *au pair* girl? It is not a very settled life. I thought Englishwomen were more ambitious.'

'I want to see as much of the world as possible before I settle down to dull routine,' Diana retorted. 'Anyway, as I said, I'm twenty-three, *British*,' she emphasised the word, 'my parents live in Bothwell, in Scotland. I like reading, travelling, animals and meeting people. I hate horror films, spiders, unexplained mysteries, and—and I'm terribly superstitious.' At this confession she gave a self-deprecating little laugh, a soft, throaty sound with an appealing catch in it. 'My family and friends always say it will lead me into trouble some day.'

He leaned forward in his chair and Diana almost flinched as long olive-skinned fingers stretched out towards her. But it was only to examine the good luck charm about her neck.

Even so, it brought him too close for comfort, and she was aware of her unconfined breasts rising and falling in a rapid little breath. He had noticed her agitation and for a moment his eyes rested interestedly on the swelling curves, and to her horror Diana realised that her nipples had become hard little peaks beneath the tight material. Never in her life had she been so responsive to a man's sexual appraisal.

But it was not about the amulet or her unwanted, unexpected reaction to him, thank goodness, that he commented. His eyes were on her hands now.

'And you are not married?' he asked.

'No.'

'And you are not engaged?'

'No.'

'There is *no* man in your life?'

'Not at the moment.' Diana had recently broken with someone she had been dating for over a year. David had become increasingly possessive and jealous, not only of her but of her time. He had resented the fact that her job took her away so much. And finally Diana had realised that he had destroyed her affection for him.

At the moment she was free and rather enjoying the sense of being her own mistress once more. She would like to marry some day, obviously, but right now she was in no particular hurry to find another boyfriend.

'So if I were to employ you as my daughter's companion, you could give her your undivided attention?'

So the 'little *signorina*' *was* his daughter. Diana was beginning to wonder if she had discovered the correct Conte Ortoni. Also she felt decidedly guilty at the way she was deceiving him. But she had to go on with her deception, at least until she found out if he did know—or had known—Julia. It was no good asking him outright. If he denied all knowledge of her cousin she had no way of determining if he spoke the truth.

'I've no other commitments,' she said, but as she told the

expedient lie, she crossed two fingers behind her back in propitiation of fate.

CHAPTER TWO

SHE was holding her breath, Diana realised, as she waited for Giacomo Ortoni's decision, and she had to make a conscious effort to relax. He might become suspicious about her motives if she appeared unnaturally anxious to enter his employ.

Those unusual green eyes of his were surveying her again and it took all her self-control to sit still and not fidget under their gaze.

Finally he spread his hands in a gesture that was almost one of resignation.

'*I* am *not* superstitious, *signorina*. But I have been told that I *am* intuitive. My good sense tells me that I should send you away. And yet . . .' He stood up. 'And yet my intuition—and a certain curiosity—prompts me to employ you.'

'*Curiosity*?' Diana queried. Of all the reasons for deciding to employ someone! But he did not enlarge upon this odd statement.

'Come, I will show you my establishment and explain the house rules.'

What exactly did he mean by house rules? Diana wondered a little apprehensively, as she followed him on a tour of the Palazzo Ortoni.

They began at the top of the building. Here, as was usual for a building of its period, the kitchens were situated.

'Can you cook, *signorina*?'

'Aye, of course. Why?'

He smiled wryly.

'Because, in an all-male household . . .'

'I thought men—according to men—made the best chefs!' she riposted. 'Are you saying I'd have to cook too?'

'Do you have a strong objection to doing so?'

'N-no,' she said hastily. It wasn't what she'd envisaged, certainly. But she didn't want to give the Conte a reason not to employ her.

'Myself, I do not eat at home very often,' he told her. 'But you will need to prepare your own food and that of your charge.' His mouth twisted still more. 'Or eat Tomaso's cooking.'

Giacomo Ortoni certainly didn't live in style. If it were not for the size and the furnishings of the *palazzo* it would be difficult to believe he was a wealthy man of rank.

'Why,' Diana asked impulsively, 'do you have an all-male household, Conte Ortoni?'

At once his expression became closed.

'Because that is how it suits me.' He was haughty, very much the *grand seigneur*, forbidding further questions on the subject. 'And *signore* will suffice when you address me,' he told her. 'It is only my own people who address me as *Conte.*'

As they continued their tour, Diana was impressed by the magnificence of the rooms through which they passed, including a suite which would be hers—if she decided to take the job, he told her. The way he put it sounded as though he thought she might have changed her mind.

'Of course I'll take it,' she said firmly.

'You have not yet heard all the conditions,' he reminded her. 'You have references to show me?'

'Er . . . no. As I told your man, I was in Florence and came on the off-chance.'

He looked at her consideringly.

'Normally I would not employ anyone without first seeing their references. However, I flatter myself on being a good judge of character. But you will send for your references, of course.' Then, before she could reply, 'You have luggage with you?'

'I left it at the Pensione Leonardo. When would you like me to start?'

'Now,' he surprised her by saying. 'If you take the job you will begin now. Write a note to the proprietor of the Leonardo and Tomaso will fetch your belongings.'

'Och, there's no need for that,' she protested. 'I can quite easily . . .'

'*Signorina*,' the hand he placed on her arm effectively silenced her, stirring inside her a quickening response that she preferred not to name. 'I said you had not heard all my conditions. If you take this job you will not return to the *pensione*. You will remain here now. And while you are in my employ you will go nowhere unescorted.'

'You mean I can't leave the *palazzo*?' She stared at him disbelievingly.

'Not unless you are accompanied either by Tomaso, or by myself and my other men. Do you agree?'

Diana was about to protest violently when she caught a gleam in the vivid green eyes. If she refused to accept his ruling she would receive her *congé*—now. And any chance of finding out anything about the missing Julia would be lost. She swallowed, though it cost her a considerable effort to say meekly, 'All right. I agree.'

But it was a little worrying, she thought, when Tomaso, her letter of explanation in his pocket, had left for the *pensione*. She had expected to have time to make her own arrangements and in particular to write a letter home, telling her family of her whereabouts.

Now a nervous ripple zipped down her spine as she recalled how Julia had suddenly failed to communicate with *her* parents. Suppose Aunt Marion's fears about her daughter were correct? Suppose she, Diana, were also to mysteriously disappear?

In an attempt to stifle her nerves, she questioned the Conte.

'When do I get to meet your daughter, *signore*? And is there anything in particular that I should know about her?'

'Now that I am engaging you as Maria's companion I will send for her.' He didn't offer any explanation of where the child had been in the meantime. His tone became dry. 'Since Tomaso has already been so free with his information, you will have gathered she is not an easy child to handle.'

'Does she have any . . . any special problems?' Diana asked when he had been silent for a moment or two.

'My daughter,' his shoulders lifted in a heavy sigh accompanied by a characteristically Latin spreading of the hands, 'has many problems, Signorina Watt, including the fact that since her accident she is unable to walk and rarely speaks.'

'Brain damage?' Diana queried.

'I think not. I believe her condition to be psychosomatic.'

'Then how on earth am I supposed to teach her English?' Diana exclaimed. 'She sounds more like a case for therapy, or a psychiatrist even.'

'Do you think I have not tried such remedies?' he rasped. His dark face was fierce, hawklike in its aquiline beauty. 'The medicos have washed their hands of her. Without exception they all say there is no reason why she should not walk and talk like any other child. I have little faith in the medical profession.'

'How old is she?'

'Eleven.'

'And how long has she been this way? You said she had an accident?'

'She had a fall a few years ago. Before that she was a perfectly healthy, normal child.'

Diana hesitated before she asked her next question.

'Her mother? Your . . . your wife . . ?'

'Maria's mother is dead,' he said shortly, and his features contorted—with grief? Anger? Diana wasn't sure.

'And . . . and she doesn't have a stepmother?' Somehow she hated herself for probing, but she had to do it.

'No!' There was no mistaking the emotion now. It was anger. But Diana was too puzzled to heed his anger. If Maria had no stepmother, what had become of Julia? A thrill of fear ran down her spine and even the cool, familiar touch of her good-luck charm failed to reassure her.

Abruptly Giacomo Ortoni stood up.

'You must excuse me, *signorina*,' he said, still stiffly displeased. 'I have urgent affairs in the city. Please consider the Palazzo Ortoni your home. If you have any urgent needs Tomaso will be back shortly. You realise he speaks no English?'

'That's all right. I know enough Italian to make him understand.' Diana blushed slightly at the understatement. 'But when . . . when will *you* be back?' She wasn't normally of a nervous disposition, but on their tour of the *palazzo* they had met no one else. It was a large building and despite its rich furnishings a rather sombre place. A sinister air was added by the presence of the unprepossessing Tomaso. It

38 THE EAGLE OF SOLAMENZA

didn't strike her just at that moment how odd it was that
she should find the Conte's presence reassuring rather than
otherwise.

His eyebrows assumed a sardonic arch and at once Diana
knew she had overstepped the invisible but very real
boundary between employer and employee.

'I assure you, *signorina*, you will not lack for my society.
Indeed, you may even tire of it. *Addio!*' And before she
could think of a suitable retort he was gone.

With Giacomo Ortoni's departure Diana was at
something of a loss. It was difficult in someone else's home
to know how to pass the time. Still, Giacomo had made her
free of its facilities and, realising that it was some time since
she had eaten, she made her way upstairs once more to the
kitchen. The Conte had said he rarely ate at home, and a
few minutes' examination of the kitchen cupboards
confirmed that statement. No man of his obvious taste and
discernment would be satisfied with the sketchy menu
provided here. Tomaso's choice, no doubt. That would
have to be remedied, if she were to take over the cooking for
herself and her charge. While she waited for some pasta to
cook Diana hunted out a notebook from her handbag and
began to make a shopping list.

She was still eating when Tomaso returned. He entered
the kitchen, obviously in search of food for himself, and
Diana thought he regarded her heaped plate rather
wistfully. She addressed him in his own language.

'If I'd known how long you'd be I'd have cooked for you
too,' she told him. She handed him the list of provisions.
'Signor Ortoni said to ask you for anything I needed. How
soon could you get these?'

'After *siesta*,' he grunted in a surly tone. 'All shops are
shut now for *siesta*.'

Diana had quite forgotten that it was that sacred moment of the Italian afternoon when the population was horizontal. So what business could the Conte be conducting in the city?

Though she didn't care for his manner, Diana was determined not to show any reaction and went on calmly eating her lunch while she considered how to gain the large man's confidence. She would have to use anyone and everyone if she were to discover anything about her missing cousin. She decided on a roundabout approach.

'The Conte tells me his daughter is away,' she said as Tomaso began to prepare food for himself. 'Has she been on holiday?'

'Holiday?' His expression was scornful. 'No. At a school for the handicapped, run by nuns.' And, with a sneer on his ugly face, 'The Conte thought she would be safer there.'

'Safer? In what way? I don't understand.'

Again he looked at her as though she were ignorant.

'*L'Aquila* has enemies. The family and household of rich men are always at risk. Kidnapping is an Italian trade.'

L'Aquila—the Eagle. Diana asked him why he called his employer that. The big man shrugged.

'*Chi lo sa*? Who knows?' The expression was accompanied by a lifting and dropping of the arms. 'It is what I have heard his people call him, "The Eagle of Solamenza".'

'Aren't *you* from Solamenza, then?'

'Me?' He sounded affronted. 'That backwater? I am a Roman. Now Luca and Ubaldo, *they* are peasants, they are from Solamenza.'

'Luca and Ubaldo?' she queried.

'His other bodyguards.'

She should have known—the heavy, muscular body, the pugilistic features. But Giacomo Ortoni must be very important or very wealthy, or both, to need such protection. She wondered why, if his daughter were at risk from kidnappers, he did not leave her in safety in his Abruzzi retreat. And Tomaso had said that members of his household were vulnerable too. She supposed the 'household' could now be said to include herself. What had she got herself into? Suddenly she lost her appetite. She stood up and scraped the rest of the pasta away and to quell her nerves began a vigorous attack on the far from pristine kitchen. Tomaso's doubtful domestic skills obviously didn't include cleaning. She'd noticed, during her tour of the *palazzo*, that the fine furnishings all carried an undisturbed layer of dust.

'Surely the Conte could have some of the local women in to do some housework,' she said disgustedly.

'Women chatter,' said Tomaso with a fine disregard for his own recent revelations. 'The Conte does not like talk in the city.' Tomaso's meal was ready and he sat down at the kitchen table, shovelling great forkfuls of the pasta into his wide gap-toothed mouth. He had unfolded a newspaper, perhaps as a hint against further interrogation, and Diana decided not to push her luck. There would be other opportunities to question the bodyguard. She decided to go and unpack.

Although she wasn't too sure that she liked the gloomy *palazzo*, Diana couldn't fault her room. Gleaming hardwood floors set off richly woven rugs and ivory-inlaid furniture. A carved arched doorway linked the sitting-room to a spacious bedroom, high-ceilinged with a large, old-fashioned but pristine marble bathroom.

Once her clothes had been hung in the vast wardrobe and her cosmetics set out on the marble-topped vanity unit, Diana was restless again. Despite the saying 'when in Rome do as the Romans do', she had never observed the *siesta* period. Then she recalled that during their tour of the *palazzo*, Giacomo Ortoni had told her she might make use of his well-stocked library.

'There are many volumes of English literature,' he had told her, and it had suited Diana not to tell him that she could read Italian as easily as her own language.

The library, like most of the rooms in the *palazzo*, required artificial lighting even during the day. Again the floors were of polished hardwood and shelves lined the whole of one wall from floor to ceiling. Another wall held more portraits. Some of these were of women, as dark and haughty and good-looking as their Ortoni menfolk. And the third wall framed maps of obvious antiquity. Comfortable, well-used leather armchairs suggested that this was the Conte's favourite room in the house.

Diana scanned the bookshelves. It wasn't difficult to spot the English volumes; there was a special section reserved for them. She would probably borrow something to read in bed tonight, but for the moment she was more interested in the rest of Giacomo Ortoni's library. There were sections devoted to religious, scientific and political subjects. And one shelf, she soon discovered, was devoted to a history of the Ortoni family. The leather-bound volumes set at a convenient eye-level for a tall man were just within her reach. She had just taken down the first in the series when the sound of a footfall on the uncarpeted floor made her swing around.

Although Giacomo Ortoni had given her permission to use his library she felt as though she had been caught red-handed in some misdemeanour. He came towards her and held out a long-fingered olive hand for the book she held, and as he took it his fingers brushed hers. The touch sent tiny shocks pulsing up her arm.

'I think you will find this a little beyond you,' he observed as Diana sought to subdue the effects of that contact. 'It is part of my family history.'

'I did manage to make out that much!' The unwanted sensations had given a slight edge to her voice and her legs felt oddly tremulous.

'And you are interested?' He sounded surprised.

'Why not?' she said, still on the defensive. 'Since I'm going to work for you I thought . . .'

'What would you like to know about my family, *signorina?*'

A hell of a lot, she brooded, including your relationship with my cousin Julia and her whereabouts. But she kept that particular thought to herself. She shrugged.

'I don't know—something, anything. But if you don't want me to . . .'

'I should be pleased to relate our family history for you. Sit down!' He indicated one of the capacious leather chairs and, as her legs still felt decidedly shaky, she obeyed him.

He chose to remain standing, leaning against the hide-covered desk, his long legs crossed at the ankles. He did not open the book he had taken from her but held it in his hands, turning it over and over. For such a strongly masculine man he had long, sensitive fingers, and these caressed the binding and the gold lettering as he spoke.

'As you will have guessed from the number of volumes on the subject, my family goes back a long way. To the Norman conquest of Southern Italy, in fact. Do you know anything about Italian history?'

'The conquest was 1036,' she told him, and felt a little ripple of satisfaction as his eyebrows indicated his surprise.

'I am impressed, *signorina*!' he commented, then, 'The first Ortoni recorded in Italian history were Rainulf and his twin brother Tancred. But there was not the closeness between them that one might expect of twins. Rainulf was the older by half an hour, and Tancred resented this. Each brother went his own way, founded his own dynasty—the beginning of a family feud which lasts until this day.'

'Which one are you descended from?' Diana asked.

'Rainulf. Within ten years of their arrival in Italy both Rainulf and Tancred were famous and wealthy men. When the conquest was over both brothers built themselves mountain fastnesses in the Abruzzi and became robber barons, the terror of the district. They weren't the only ones by any means. There were hundreds of robber chiefs, but the Ortoni twins were by far the most successful. And, not content with preying on others, they continually besieged each other.'

'When did your family become "respectable"?' Diana asked, and saw a gleam of amusement light Giacomo Ortoni's eyes.

'Not until a few centuries later when one of Rainulf's descendants, the first Giacomo, was made Conte of Solamenza. Tancred's branch of the family did not gain respectability quite as soon and never achieved a title—another cause of bitterness.'

'And since then?' she asked.

Giacomo shrugged almost deprecatingly.

'My branch of the Ortoni family has always been respected. There have always been Ortonis in politics and in the church. One of my cousins is an ordained priest, another a minister in our present government.'

'And you?'

'Among other things I am the *primogenito*, the first-born, the head of our family.' It was said not with conceit but with great matter-of-factness. 'It carries responsibilities.'

Diana presumed that meant he didn't work. She supposed there was no point if he was rich.

'What on earth do you find to do with yourself?' she asked, and then, almost accusingly, 'You said you had "business" in the city.'

'I do not discuss my business, Signorina Watt, but I assure you my time is adequately filled.' It was not unpleasantly said, but Diana felt snubbed. 'You may be interested to know,' he went on, 'that I have sent for Maria. She will be here tomorrow evening.'

Diana was quite unprepared for her first sight of Maria Ortoni when they met in the grand *salone* next evening.

She had expected the child to resemble her father in looks and colouring, especially since seeing the portraits of the female Ortonis. Dark, every one of them. Julia's portrait would not have looked out of place in their company, for her cousin had been a striking brunette. Uneasily, Diana registered that fact that when she thought about Julia it was always in the past tense.

The only point of resemblance she could detect between Maria and her father was their green eyes. The child had a pointed, heart-shaped face, pale-skinned and freckled, framed by a cloud of red-gold hair.

'Oh, how pretty you are!' Diana could not help exclaiming, and was startled by the glint of pure malevolence that flickered in the child's eyes. The shock made her forget to guard her tongue, and impulsively, to Giacomo, she said, 'Maria must resemble her mother?'

He said nothing, merely inclining his handsome head, and there was no doubt this time that his expression held pain. Yet it was an anguish mingled with love, she thought, as he looked down at his daughter in her wheelchair. And Diana was seized with a sudden unexpected yearning to be able to help, even to comfort this proud but obviously unhappy man.

'Won't you welcome Signorina Watt to Florence, *bambina mia*?' Giacomo said gently. 'You are mistress of the *palazzo* and it is your place to do so.'

But the child's only response was a surly expression, her eyes expressing dumb insolence.

'Perhaps it would be better if you left Maria and me to get acquainted on our own?' Diana suggested. 'I've often noticed that bairns play up more in front of their parents.'

'*Bairns*?' he queried.

'Och,' she said apologetically, 'it's a Scottish word. It just means "children". I usually try not to use such expressions when I'm with people who don't understand. I'm sorry.' Then she asked him, 'Would you mind leaving us alone together?'

'As you wish.' He was obviously still mortified by his daughter's behaviour. He turned to leave the *salone*, then paused in the doorway. 'I must tell you, *signorina*, that I do not hold out much hope of you being any more successful than Maria's former companions. If we were . . .' he hesitated, 'an ordinary family I suppose I would have left her at the convent. But it has become fraught with too many difficulties—too much risk.'

'The risk of kidnapping?' asked Diana. 'Tomaso said . . .'

'Tomaso again!' he said irritably. 'I must speak to Tomaso. I do not tolerate employees who gossip.'

Diana felt the implied reprimand and her gamine little features coloured. Nevertheless she knew she would take any and every opportunity to find out what she could about Giacomo Ortoni and his family affairs. And to herself she had to confess that her interest was not solely confined to Julia's welfare. Giacomo Ortoni excited her curiosity in more ways than one.

She even found herself hoping that the story of his involvement with her cousin had been unfounded, or at least that there had been no sinister implications. Beneath his autocratic reserve she thought she sensed a likeable man, and certainly—she sighed a little wistfully—he was a very attractive one.

With the Conte's departure she turned to look consideringly at Maria. The child was still regarding her with a hostile stare, and Diana felt that the best way to cope with her enmity was to remain unruffled by it. She sat down in a chair a little distance away from the wheelchair and began to talk in a friendly, conversational manner.

'Florence is a beautiful city. I've always wanted to spend more time here. I expect you know a lot more about it than I do. But perhaps with your father's permission we'll be able to do a little sightseeing.'

It was a little disconcerting speaking to an unresponsive, unfriendly audience. It was almost as if she were talking to herself, but Diana persevered.

'I believe your father has another home, at Solamenza? I wonder if it's anything like this *palazzo*?'

For a moment a look of ineffable scorn transformed the child's pale, piquant features, and Diana had the distinct

impression that she was about to say something. But the
moment passed. Diana decided to try another tack.

'Do you know, I think I'm going to enjoy your company.'
And as the child's face expressed mocking disbelief, she
nodded. 'You see, I love to talk, but so do most other
people, and sometimes it's difficult to get a word in
edgeways. With you I'll be able to talk all the time, won't
I?'

If it hadn't been pathetic the struggle going on within the
child would have been amusing, as the desire for conflict
fought with her stubbornly maintained silence. Then, in a
harsh croak, as though the rarely used voice were a rusty
instrument, Maria spoke—and, astonishingly, in heavily
accented but very passable English.

'I can talk perfectly well if I want to. I just don't
choose to. Especially,' the tone became venomous, 'to my
father.'

Any satisfaction Diana might have felt at the results of
her ploy was swamped by shocked surprise. She had
imagined that the child's aura of hostility had been for her
alone. But now it seemed most of it had been directed
towards Giacomo Ortoni.

'But why on earth,' she demanded, 'shouldn't you want
to speak to your own father?'

'I have my reasons,' the child said with an adult air so
reminiscent of her aristocratic, autocratic father that Diana
had difficulty repressing a smile. 'Actually,' Maria went on,
'it's been rather boring not talking to anyone. I might,'
condescendingly, 'talk to you—if you promise not to give
me away. *Do* you promise?' she demanded fiercely.

Diana demurred. 'It doesn't seem very fair to your
father.'

It was almost frightening the way the child's face

contorted into an expression that Diana had no difficulty in interpreting. What on earth had Giacomo Ortoni done to incur such hatred?

'If you don't promise not to tell him I won't speak to you either,' Maria threatened.

It might be worth while going along with the child's demands, for the present at least, Diana decided.

'Then I promise,' she said. 'But when you say you don't talk to *anyone*, do you mean not even when you were at the convent?'

'Of course not,' scornfully, 'they would have immediately told my father.'

'What about when you visit Solamenza? To the rest of your family?'

'They are *not* my family,' the child said fiercely. 'They are all Ortonis. You can see that I am not. I am like my mother's family. Besides,' she added in a flatter tone, 'if you don't talk you hear more.'

Really she was the most amazing eleven-year-old. Diana couldn't remember meeting such an adult-mannered pre-teenager.

'If people think you can't talk,' Maria went on, 'they think you're stupid, that you can't hear either. I hear a lot.'

Strangely, that fact didn't seem to afford Maria much satisfaction, and Diana guessed that some of the things she overheard made her unhappy.

Once Maria had begun to talk it was as if a long-dammed torrent had been released, and the child continued to chatter, asking questions about England as Diana helped her undress and then put her to bed. Maria admired Diana's dress, the blue of which was an exact match for her eyes, asking if it were real silk. But she did not volunteer any more information about herself or her family.

'Tell me something, Maria,' said Diana, 'you pretend to everyone that you can't talk . . .' Then she hesitated, wondering if she ought to put her thoughts into words. But the child was astute.

'You want to know if I'm *pretending* I can't walk?' And as Diana nodded uncomfortably, 'Well, I'm *not. I'm not!*' she repeated. 'Do you think I like being stuck in that chair?' Her green eyes stared, hugely tragic, out of the heart-shaped face and her lips trembled. Yet something in her expression forbade Diana to pity her and she checked her involuntary movement to take the child in her arms.

'Did you make any headway with Maria?' was Giacomo Ortoni's inevitable question. Diana was in the kitchen preparing herself an evening meal when he came in search of her. The anxious appeal in his face and voice made Diana wish she were not bound by her promise to his daughter.

'It's early days yet,' she said evasively.

The hope in his eyes vanished, dulling their brilliant green. He sighed hugely.

'I had thought she might respond to an Englishwoman.'

'Why an Englishwoman?' Diana queried.

There was pain in his throaty voice.

'Maria's mother, my wife, was British. British? English? It is all the same, *si*?'

'Well, not quite,' said Diana.

Giacomo dismissed this with a gesture.

'In any event, Maria and her mother were very close. The more so perhaps because my . . . my affairs frequently take me away from home.'

Diana couldn't help wondering if he meant 'affairs' in the literal sense. There had to be some reason for the child's antagonism towards her father. But then surely the child was too young to be aware of such things? And Giacomo Ortoni's whole manner was expressive of grief when he spoke of his late wife. She glanced at him. He was leaning, hands in trouser pockets, against the edge of the kitchen table, and again she mused on how little style he kept. How many men of rank would be found in the kitchen, conversing with the hired help? He looked tired, too—though she couldn't be sure whether it was a physical fatigue or a weariness of spirit.

'Have you eaten?' she asked impulsively. 'Would you like me to cook something for you . . . ?' At the expression of doubt on his face her voice faltered away. He rarely ate at home, he had said. He was probably accustomed to *haute cuisine* meals. And Diana knew that her cooking fell into the good but plain and wholesome category.

But apparently his doubt wasn't for her skill.

'You would not mind? I usually dine at a local restaurant, but I must confess, tonight I am not in the mood for eating out. Besides which I have given Luca and Ubaldo the evening off. And Tomaso's place is here at the *palazzo*, with Maria.'

'Luca and Ubaldo, your bodyguards,' Diana said as she began to add extra ingredients to her saucepans. 'Tomaso told me about them. Do you really have to take them everywhere you go?'

He nodded, but for a moment a proud lift of his dark head dispelled the weariness.

'Not for my own sake, you understand, *signorina*? I am not afraid for my own safety. But if I were to fall into the wrong hands it could prove a threat to other members of my family.'

'You mean these people would hold you to ransom?'

'Yes,' his aquiline features were grim. 'And Ortoni

money is not to be utilised for such purposes.'

Diana waited expectantly, but the Conte did not seem inclined to tell her just how his money *should* be used. He had two homes to support, of course. He had described himself as the 'head of the family'. Perhaps he also had dependent relatives; old families often had.

'How do you like your steak?' she asked him when it was obvious the silence was not going to be broken.

'*A puntino*—medium.' The thought of food seemed to lighten Giacomo's mood. A smile transformed his grave features and something inside Diana twisted oddly, a sensation that was almost pain. 'It smells good,' he told her. Then, 'You will share a bottle of wine with me?'

She smiled back.

'I don't know about sharing a bottle,' she told him. 'One glass, perhaps. And even that usually goes to my head!'

Perhaps it was the wine—Diana drank only on rare occasions and Giacomo Ortoni, despite her protests, insisted on topping up her glass—but to her there was an air almost of unreality about their *al fresco* meal. Eating together, seated on hard, unpretentious wooden chairs, at the small kitchen table which Diana had recently scrubbed, gave the occasion a sense of intimacy. And as they talked easily on a variety of subjects she began to feel as if she had known the Conte for years. When she had first met him—was it really only yesterday?—he had seemed cold and remote, with all the hauteur one would expect of a nobleman. Since Maria's return—and this evening in particular—his initial curt barriers had broken down and he seemed much more approachable. She didn't feel a bit in awe of him. In fact—she regarded him a little hazily, very much aware of his good looks and vibrant masculinity—if she'd met him in other circumstances . . .

'*Signorina*?' He was looking at her a little quizzically.

'You know,' she told him huskily, 'I wouldn't mind if you called me Diana. I'm not used to so much formality.'

He didn't answer immediately but just went on looking at her, an unfathomable expression in his green eyes, and Diana thought that perhaps, encouraged by his friendly manner, she had overstepped the mark. He might think she expected him to return the compliment, and to be truthful she couldn't quite see herself calling him Giacomo. Feeling embarrassed, she stood up, intending the clear the table, and the next moment found herself sprawling across Giacomo Ortoni's knees.

'I . . . I'm sorry,' she struggled to regain her balance. 'I suddenly felt giddy. It . . . it must be the wine. I'm not used to . . .' The words stuck suddenly in her throat, for Giacomo's arms had closed about her and he was regarding her very oddly—very oddly indeed.

Diana tried to avert her eyes and found that she couldn't. Her head still felt dizzy and her heart hammered in her throat. She was conscious that the soft silky folds of her draped bodice had parted, exposing too much of the soft curves of her breasts. She saw his nostrils flare. Then he was kissing her with a hard demanding fierceness that could not be denied.

At first she struggled. His passion was so instant, frightening. But it was exciting too, and Diana knew she was already fascinated by him, drawn to his enigmatic personality, responsive to the strong sexuality she had sensed in him—a sexuality that was now to the fore.

He held her close, his imprisoning arms so tight about her that she could scarcely breathe. His kisses were sending shock-waves of ecstasy through her veins. His hands began to caress her, outlining her body with sensuous expertise, and she felt heavily lethargic, unable to move to stop him, lost in the wonder of the sensation aroused by his exploring lips as they moved down the column of her neck and found the exposed curves of her breasts.

But as his caresses threatened to become more intimate a spark of sanity rose through the stupor of wine and kisses. Good heavens, she'd only known this man five minutes! What did he think he was doing? Worse, what did she think *she* was doing, letting him behave this way? She renewed her resistance, twisting her head from side to side, hammering at his chest with her small clenched fists.

'Stop it!' she gasped. 'Stop it! Let go of me!'

At first he fought back, trying to restrain her, trying in vain to recapture her lips, to subjugate her once more by his passion. But Diana was not to be wooed again, and at last he let her go.

She stumbled to her feet and backed away from him, her blue eyes blazing with anger.

Giacomo rose to his feet to confront her and before she could speak, 'Spare me the outrage, *signorina*.' His tone was cynical. 'You received no more than you asked for.'

'I? Asked for?' she gasped.

He moved towards her, tall, almost menacing.

'I am disappointed in you, *signorina*. I *had* thought perhaps there was more to you than the usual run of girls who have applied for this post. But there is always this forwardness in the Englishwomen who come here as *au pairs*, and your whole attitude this evening has been one of invitation, has it not?'

'No!' Diana snapped. 'It most certainly hasn't!'

'No?' he enquired sardonically. 'Your feigned attack of

giddiness . . .'

'No,' she said again. The arrogance of the man to think she'd throw herself at him like that! 'I *wasn't* pretending—I really did lose my balance. I told you I had no head for wine. I don't know what sort of *English* girls you've met—the wrong sort, obviously. But I'm *Scottish*, and Scottish girls don't . . . at least *this* one doesn't . . .'

'You let me kiss you,' he pointed out. He was very close now and Diana passed a nervous tongue over dry lips. 'You returned my kisses.'

Unfortunately that was undeniable. She had no answer for him, but he went on anyway. 'The meal—you *were* anxious for me to spend the evening with you!'

'No,' Diana felt on surer ground now, 'I offered to cook for you because I felt sorry for you, that's all.'

Unwittingly she had uttered the ultimate turn-off, the unforgivable. Giacomo Ortoni's head had been inclined towards her almost as if he would renew his passionate onslaught. Now he snapped upright, his dark brows drawing together in an angry frown.

'*You* felt sorry for *me?*' His tone dared her to repeat the insult. But Diana was no coward.

'You looked tired,' she said steadily, 'you were upset about your daughter. It must be difficult, not having a wife to . . . I just wanted to . . .' She bit her lip. She'd been on the point of saying she wanted to comfort him, but that was a statement capable of wider interpretation, and with each word she seemed to be offending him further.

'You can spare me your excuses, *signorina, and* your pity! I am not interested in either.' And as she shrank from the ice in his face and voice he turned on his heel and stalked—there was no other way of describing it—out of the kitchen.

Diana drew in a deep unsteady breath and sank down on to one of the wooden chairs. She sat there for some time, trying to analyse her tattered feelings, the confusion of sentiments that Giacomo Ortoni had stirred in her. There was the rush of tender concern she had felt for him which had made her so vulnerable to his kisses, and now she was left on an emotional high, unsatisfied, her own longing and anger mingled. Until today no other man had ever affected her in this way. But she didn't want to probe too deeply into that thought, afraid of what it might reveal.

At last she rose and made her way to her own room. As she undressed and showered she tried to will herself to think of other things—of how she might be able to help Maria—of her mission here to see what she could discover about her cousin Julia. But despite her brain's desperate battle to keep control she could not erase the memory of Giacomo Ortoni's kisses, nor temper her body's treacherous longing to lie in his arms once more.

CHAPTER THREE

'*BUON giorno, signorina*! *Buon giorno*, Maria!' Giacomo Ortoni saluted Diana with cool urbanity, but there was a warmer, pleading note in his voice as he addressed his daughter.

Diana had been dreading her next encounter with the Conte. She had had no idea what his manner towards her would be. She wasn't altogether sure what her own attitude should be. Obviously he had opted for cold politeness, and so she followed his lead.

'Good morning, *signore*.'

Maria, of course, made no response to her father's greeting, and Diana saw the quickly concealed hurt in his eyes.

'Have you any plans for today, *signorina*?' he asked.

Diana had plenty. She had spent a considerable time working out an itinerary that would keep her and Maria away from the *palazzo* for several hours, thus avoiding Giacomo's disturbing presence. Her conversation with the child the previous evening had elicited the information that Maria had seen very little of Florence.

'Well, you can't expect people to take you out if you don't ask,' Diana had pointed out. Now she told Giacomo, 'There are several places I should like to take Maria—with your permission, of course. I suppose Tomaso does have to go with us?' she asked with a touch of wistfulness in her soft Scottish voice. It would have been so much more pleasant to roam at will with only the child for company.

'Not only Tomaso,' Giacomo Ortoni told her, 'but Luca and Ubaldo also. For I too shall accompany you.'

'Oh!' And after all her scheming to avoid him!

Diana's dismay must have shown in her face, for he went on, 'I see the idea displeases you, but I did warn you that I . . .'

'Och, no,' she said hastily. 'I'm just surprised that you can spare the time.'

'Today I have no previous engagements.'

As the Conte had remarked yesterday, it *was* a pity Maria did not come from an ordinary family, Diana reflected as they set out from the *palazzo*. Alone with Diana the child would have gained more enjoyment from the outing. As it was, Maria lapsed into a sullen silence which she stubbornly maintained all day.

Diana tried to behave naturally, making comments to the child on all that they saw, but, gaining no response, she was forced more and more into conversation with Giacomo Ortoni. Then too she was continually aware of the trio of bodyguards at only a stride's distance behind them, their eyes and ears constantly on the alert for any unauthorised approach.

But even so none of these disadvantages could spoil Florence for her. 'La bella Firenze' was a place of bridges—those crossing the yellow turbulent waters of the River Arno. Diana had visited the Ponte Vecchio before and drooled over the silversmiths' and jewellers' shops that lined both sides of the world-famous bridge. She had window-shopped—all she could afford—in the Via Tornabuoni, a most elegant street, the epitome of high-class shopping. Every building, ancient and modern alike, the shops with their beautiful displays, all wore the mantle of

Florentine elegance.

The city was small and compact, making it easy to explore, since most things of interest were within easy walking distance. But the cobbles and narrow pavements meant that Florence was not for anyone hampered by a wheelchair, and Diana suggested that they go to the Boboli Gardens. She had never had time to include the gardens in previous itineraries.

'Och!' she exclaimed, her Scottish accent becoming more pronounced as it always did in moments of strong emotion, 'they're like something out of an old-fashioned picture book—too magnificent to be real!'

Giacomo Ortoni seemed gratified by her admiration.

'The gardens were created in the sixteenth century for Cosimo the First. One of my ancestors had a hand in their design.'

'One of the respectable ones, of course?' Since his mood seemed to have mellowed, Diana dared to tease him, and was rewarded by that flashing smile that did strange things to her knees.

'But of course.'

The gardens climbed the hill behind the Pitti Palace to the city's southern walls. Constructed in the highly elaborate Mannerist style, they consisted of a vast and beautiful park full of fancies and follies—fountains, grottoes and statues. Even Maria could not repress a smile at the fountain which showed a fat dwarf astride a tortoise.

Giacomo suggested that Diana might like to see inside one of the caves. 'Alas, it is not possible to take the wheelchair inside, but it would be a pity for you to miss the experience.'

'This is known as Buontalenti's grotto,' he said. He had accompanied her, leaving the three bodyguards watching over Maria.

It was early and there had not been many sightseers in the gardens, and Diana was acutely aware that they had the cave to themselves. Stupid to be so nervous. She took a deep, steadying breath.

'Watch your step,' his hand grasped her elbow, his fingers warm and hard through the sleeve of her dress, 'the ground is uneven.'

She tried hard to ignore the sensations his proximity was causing and to concentrate on the grotto's décor—casts of Michelangelo's Slaves emerging from the rough cave walls.

'The originals are in the Accademia, of course,' Giacomo told her. Then: 'Once upon a time visitors here would have been drenched with water by practical joke devices. But they are no longer active.'

The grotto consisted of three chambers. In the farthest one stood a beautiful statue. Diana recognised the classical pose.

'Venus, the Goddess of Love!' she exclaimed. 'What on earth is she doing here?'

'Perhaps the designer hoped that lovers visiting the grotto would be inspired by her presence,' Giacomo suggested. There was a strange note in his voice. His hand was still at her elbow and she thought its grasp tightened a little. She had never in the whole of her life been prone to claustrophobia, but now she felt suffocated, with an urgent need to be in the open. Her breasts rose and fell agitatedly as she strove to draw air into her suddenly straining lungs.

'Could . . . could we go now?' she gasped, but Giacomo's hand restrained her.

'A moment, please, *signorina*. I wish to speak to you, and this is the first time today we have been alone.'

Oh, lord, surely he wasn't going to follow up the pass

he'd made last night? In spite of his manner afterwards, the things he had said, Diana knew she was still violently attracted to him and she didn't want that attraction to get out of hand. She could not hide her alarm.

'Oh, please, I . . .'

'You are surely not afraid of me, *signorina*?' he asked incredulously, then, 'But perhaps after last evening you have reason. It is of that I wish to speak.'

'I'd rather forget about it,' Diana interrupted hastily.

'I too,' he surprised her by agreeing. And then, astonishing her still more so that she stared up at him, her lovely blue eyes wide, 'but first you will allow me to apologise for my behaviour? *Molto scusi, signorina!*' And as she did not reply, '*Signorina*? Diana? You will forgive me? You will permit that I use your name?'

Diana gathered her wits.

'I thought you saw *that* as part of my "open invitation",' she said rather bitterly.

'I was wrong. I misjudged you. I spoke in haste, in anger. As I told you, my encounters with your countrywomen have not always been pleasant. And,' he smiled wryly, 'I did not, I confess, like being rejected.' Huskily, 'I enjoyed your kisses, Diana.'

Not half as much as she had enjoyed his. At a loss for words again, she swallowed convulsively.

'Please, Diana,' he said insistently, 'before we leave here, you will accept my apology? We can behave towards each other as civilised people once more? Perhaps we can even be friends?'

She could scarcely refuse. She didn't want to refuse. But she was a little disturbed to realise just how out of proportion was her pleasure at his wish to redeem himself in her eyes.

'Of course,' she said unsteadily.

She thought he breathed a sigh of relief.

'I would not like you to resign your position with my daughter because her father cannot conduct himself as a gentleman.'

Diana felt a sense of sickening anticlimax. Fool, she mocked herself. What did you expect? That he wanted you to stay for *his* sake? And despite his use of her name he had not offered her the same privilege.

'And now can we go?' she asked coolly. 'The others will be tired of waiting.'

Other ornamental features of the Boboli Gardens included an Egyptian obelisk, an eighteenth-century coffee house and a long avenue of cypresses running down to a moated island. And Giacomo pointed out the good views the park afforded them of Florence and its rural surroundings, but somehow Diana's enthusiasm for its beauties had waned.

That day was the first of several spent exploring the city. Sometimes the Conte accompanied them, on other occasions he was absent on business, though Diana still had no idea of what it was that occupied his time. The outings were still supervised by two, sometimes three of the bodyguards, but as the men were always at a discreet distance Diana was able to ignore their presence. And when Giacomo was absent Maria replied to her comments, albeit in a whisper that did not reach the bodyguards' ears. Diana felt she was gaining the child's trust and she resolved that, when she knew Maria better, she would ask her what made her dislike her father so much that she refused to speak to him.

But this thought reminded her that time was running out. Her two weeks' leave had nearly expired and she was no nearer to discovering anything about Julia. She would have to write to her employer, she decided. It would be an easy matter to post a letter on one of their expeditions into the city. Despite the way she and Susan joked about him 'His Nibs' had been very understanding when she had told him how she would be spending her fortnight's holiday.

'If two weeks isn't enough,' he had told her, 'drop me a line. You can have two weeks extra—unpaid, of course,' he had added hastily with typical Scots thrift.

Her despatch of a letter did not pass unremarked. She was just about to slip the envelope into a post box when long olive fingers stayed her hand. Rapidly keen eyes scanned the superscription.

'To whom are you writing, Diana? This is not a letter to your parents,' he accused.

'No.' Diana thought rapidly. 'This is to my former employer, asking for the references you wanted.' To her relief Giacomo seemed satisfied.

'And now,' he said, 'we must talk about tomorrow.'

'Tomorrow?' she queried.

'*Si*. Once a week the physiotherapist spends a day with Maria, massaging and exercising her legs. You will not be needed. No doubt you will be glad of a day free of the child?'

'I rather enjoy looking after her,' and as his eyebrows raised in polite incredulity, 'But I *was* going to ask you about time off,' Diana confessed, quite forgetting the restrictions he had placed on her comings and goings.

'Alas, that is not possible in the sense you mean. However, we can make a variation in your routine. Can you be ready early tomorrow morning?'

'I suppose so. But ready for what exactly?'

'There must be many places in Italy, besides Florence,

that you have not seen?' And as Diana nodded, 'Florence has few quiet places. It is exhausting to the sightseer. How would you like to go farther afield?'

'I would have liked it very much,' Diana sighed wistfully, 'but I'm not allowed out alone, and I don't want a day out with one of your bodyguards, thank you very much. It gives me the creeps having a great muscle-bound hulk following me everywhere I go! So I'd rather stay at the *palazzo*.'

'I sympathise,' Giacomo astonished her by saying. 'I too often feel irked by their presence. But I fear we cannot dispense with my men's services altogether.' And, astonishing her still further, 'Will you accompany me if only Luca goes and I ask him to keep at a greater distance?'

'Accompany *you*? *You* mean to go with me?'

'Of course.' He seemed surprised that she should doubt it.

'But why should you bother yourself with my entertainment? I'm only an employee.'

'Oh, come now, Diana. Surely we have progressed further than that? I thought we had agreed to be friends?'

'Aye, but . . .' She felt herself flushing—because of the intent scrutiny of his eyes, but with pleasure too.

'I concern myself also, Diana, because I wish you to enjoy Italy, because I wish you to stay. I think you have not been unhappy at the Palazzo Ortoni?'

It was true. The *palazzo*, which at first had appeared gloomy and forbidding, no longer seemed so. Subtly it had exerted its mellow fascination over her—as had its owner, Diana admitted to herself. Sometimes she couldn't believe this was really the man she had come to Italy prepared to dislike and distrust. But he was waiting for an answer to his question.

'I like your home, Signor Ortoni. I know you have your

reasons for being so security-conscious. But I would like the *palazzo* even more if I didn't feel I was a prisoner there.'

'You are no more of a prisoner there than Maria or myself,' he told her wryly. 'And . . .' again his words gave her a little glow of happiness, 'your security is as important to me as my own. But come, say you will go with me tomorrow?' And Diana found herself agreeing.

Though it was still only spring the sunlight had a white-hot brilliance when they set out next morning. Giacomo Ortoni made no comment upon Diana's appearance, but she thought she detected an approving expression in his strange green eyes and she was glad she had worn the pale yellow summer dress which fitted sleekly to her trim body. The colour enhanced the gleaming gold of her hair and set off the tan she had already acquired.

He looked heart-stoppingly attractive himself in his silk shirt and muted grey slacks topped with a well-bred, sophisticated blazer. He exuded a spicy male fragrance that pleased her senses.

'Where are we going?' she asked as they drove out of the city. Giacomo was driving himself in an Italian limousine, pale ivory and black with chromium fittings. He had kept his promise and Luca followed behind them in another equally sleek car.

'To see something of the Tuscan countryside. Italy is not all cities and architecture.'

That was a masterpiece of understatement, Diana thought as they drove through a landscape of hummocky hills, scarlet poppies, tailored vineyards and silvery olive groves. Dotted here and there were isolated old farms and villas guarded by sentinel cypresses. In the fields women worked, their heads tied in handkerchiefs, their black skirts stirred by fugitive breezes. But something was exercising her mind far more than her surroundings.

'*Signore?*' she ventured, and then, encouraged by his sideways glance and pleasant enquiring smile, 'Why are you so anxious that *I* should stay with Maria? The first day we met, you said you wanted her to have an older companion. And I get the impression that you don't like Englishwomen very much.'

'All that is quite true.' As swiftly as that, the sunshine went out of the day. Diana wished she had never sought to satisfy her curiosity and she was glad the Conte had to concentrate on his driving and could not see her face. But then he went on, 'Nevertheless, there have been so many changes, so many uncertainties in her life of late that I wish to provide stability for her. I have watched you together and she seems happier, more relaxed in your company. Luca has reported to me that at times the child seems to communicate with you.'

So the brawny men who surrounded Giacomo Ortoni were not just brainless musclemen, Diana thought a trifle uneasily, for she too had things to hide.

'Tell me, Diana,' Giacomo pressed her eagerly with another of those swift sideways glances, 'is this so? *Does* Maria speak to you?'

'Aye,' Diana sighed. So much for her promise to the child. 'She does, but *signore*,' she went on hastily before he could interrupt, 'she won't go on talking to me if she thinks you know. Please . . . you must give her time—give *me* more time to gain her confidence, to find out why she . . .' She hesitated, but Giacomo finished her sentence for her.

'To find out why she hates her own father,' he said bitterly. And as Diana made a little sound of protest, 'Oh yes, Diana, it does not require any great intelligence to know that. Though only God knows why it should be so. I swear to you, I have never mistreated the child.'

'I'm sure you haven't,' Diana said with warm conviction in her soft musical voice. 'Bairns can be strange wee things. Och,' she apologised, 'I've used that word again!'

'Please,' for an instant his hand brushed her knee and Diana felt that prickling of her skin that physical contact with him always caused, 'do not apologise. I like it. I like the way you speak. I had always thought English a harsh-sounding language, but your way of speaking it is almost as musical as my own tongue.' Then, returning to their former topic of conversation, 'I love my daughter, Diana, and it is because I am aware of Maria's hatred that, despite certain security risks, I wish to have her with me. That is not so illogical as it may sound. Apart, I have no chance of changing her image of me. I live in the hope that some day I may discover its cause and dispel it. There have been other companions, but none of them has succeeded in breaking down Maria's barriers. You, Diana, have become my hope of doing so.'

'I'll do everything I can to help,' she promised him, greatly moved by his evident sincerity. And, not for the first time, she wished she hadn't made his acquaintance under false pretences. Her eyes pricked suddenly and she turned her head aside as though to admire the countryside through which they were passing.

But the admiration became real. She had been so engrossed in their conversation that she had not noticed the passage of time or the miles. The afternoon was well advanced and they were now in mountainous country, covered in thick woods of oak and chestnut, a secret country approached by steeply climbing roads.

'I thought we would stop here and have a picnic lunch,'

Giacomo told her, and already the limousine was slowing, pulling off the narrow road and bumping over a grassy verge to a shaded spot beneath the ancient trees.

Who on earth had prepared the picnic? Diana wondered, as the Conte lifted a large hamper from the boot. She asked him and he smiled.

'I am not entirely the helpless male, Diana. There have been many occasions when I've been forced to fend for myself. I just hope you will approve of my tastes.'

Certainly she could not fault them. Giacomo had provided sliced cold meats, cheese, salad, crisp bread rolls and fruit. There were *bocconotti* too—sweet pastries filled with aromatic jam, and a bottle of sparklingly clear white wine which this time, Diana resolved, she would drink of sparingly.

'How do you like the Tuscan countryside?' asked Giacomo when they had settled themselves to eat.

'Very much.'

'How does it compare with your own country? Tell me about Scotland,' he invited.

'Goodness, that's a tall order! It's a bonnie place. As varied and beautiful as Italy.'

'And your climate? Italy is a bitterly cold country for a large part of the year. Freezing blasts come from the Alps, the Dolomites and the Apennines, from autumn till the late spring.'

'Aye, but the scenery makes up for it, and so does ours—the purple of the heather, the green glens. But I think it's the mountains most of all that mean Scotland to me. Somehow, standing on a mountain—quite often above the cloud level—I feel as though I'm in a spiritual world rather than a physical one.' She blushed a little as she always did when revealing her innermost feelings. 'There's a bit in the

Scriptures that puts it into words. "I will lift up mine eyes to the hills from whence comes my consolation".'

'Then, *certamente*, you will like Solamenza,' Giacomo declared with conviction.

Diana had no doubt she would, but it was very unlikely she would ever see the Ortonis' mountain fastness. She was troubled at her lack of success in discovering anything about her cousin. And she was coming to the conclusion that soon she would have to question Giacomo outright. But she dreaded the idea, especially as it meant confessing how she had deceived him.

'Why the frown?' he asked her, bringing her out of her uncomfortable reverie.

'The sun's rather strong,' she said quickly.

The heat of the day had burned the colour from the sky and she had been glad of the shade the trees provided, but there was still a glare to support her excuse. But even so, she looked for a change of subject.

The bodyguard Luca had eaten his lunch some distance away—out of earshot of their conversation.

'I feel a bit guilty about him,' Diana confessed, 'he must be awfully bored.'

'He is well paid for his *ennui*,' Giacomo said drily. 'I do not think you will hear him complaining. More wine?' he asked, holding the bottle over her empty glass. But Diana covered it with her hand.

'No, thank you . . . and no more food either. I've eaten far too much. What with that and the heat I feel quite drowsy.' Luca, she'd noticed, was already recumbent, his chest rising and falling with the steady breaths of the sleeper.

'But you do not like sleeping in the daytime,' Giacomo commented. 'I have noticed that you do not observe the *siesta*.'

'It seems such a waste of time somehow. I always think we lose enough of our lives in sleep.'

'Then let us walk. It will be cooler further inside the woods. It will refresh you.'

'What about him?' Diana looked towards the bodyguard.

'We will let him rest. We will not go far, and besides, I do not think we run much risk out here in the countryside.'

'I must admit it would be nice not to feel someone watching me all the time,' she said as they strolled under the green branching canopy of the trees.

'I too,' Giacomo admitted. 'And I know Sandra would have disliked it intensely. Sandra was my wife,' he explained at Diana's enquiring upward glance. 'She was an affectionate person, given to moments of sudden demonstrativeness. The presence of my bodyguards would have curbed her natural urges.' So he hadn't always been surrounded by security men.

'You must miss her very much,' Diana dared to say, her soft Scottish voice throaty with sympathy. Then with a glance at his taut profile, 'How . . . how long have you been alone?'

'Three years. As you say, it has been very lonely.'

'You . . . you've never considered marrying again?' she asked, thinking now of Julia.

'No—that is, not until recently. Recently I have thought I *should* marry, for Maria's sake. A girl needs a mother.'

His words left Diana unclear as to whether his recent change of heart was solely on Maria's account or whether in fact he had someone in mind for his second wife. The thought gave her a sharp stabbing sensation that she recognised for what it was: jealousy. The attraction she felt towards Giacomo—an attraction she had sworn should not get out of hand—was becoming a very real threat to her peace of mind. She decided it was time to change the subject.

'May I ask you something, *signore*?'

He stopped in his stride and looked down at her, rather quizzically, she thought.

'I had thought that by now you would think of me as Giacomo,' he told her. She *did* think of him that way, but she had never dared to call him that. 'I call you Diana,' he pointed out.

'I know, but surely that's different. You've never given me permission . . .'

'I did not realise it was necessary, but if it will make you happy . . . *per favore*, Diana, will you call me Giacomo? In fact, my closest intimates call me Como.'

Now what was that supposed to mean? She could hardly be considered an intimate. There had been an undeniable change in the atmosphere between them; his reserve had been replaced by an almost teasing familiarity. But even so . . .

Long fingers reached out and lifted her chin.

'*Dio mio*, you are blushing, Diana! Now why is that? I wonder. Surely it is not because I wish you to use my name?' She couldn't think of a satisfactory answer and he went on. 'Say it, Diana,' he commanded, his grasp of her chin tightening a little, 'Look at me. Say it. You will not find it so difficult to do.'

'Giacomo,' she said softly, but for the life of her she could not meet his eyes.

'Ah!' It was a soft exclamation. '*Grazie*! I like the sound of my name on your lips, Diana. You have a pretty voice. But you are still embarrassed, *sì*? More practice is required. This time, look at me . . . *look at me*,' he repeated.

Diana swallowed and lifted her eyes, then almost let them

drop again before the burning green intensity of his. The ascetic planes of his face were softened by some intense feeling, and she shivered convulsively.

'Say it.' His voice was husky, sending shivers down her spine.

'Giacomo,' she said obediently, but felt her cheeks burn even more.

'That is better.' His free hand moved to encircle her waist and he drew her a little closer to him, making her acutely aware of his body warmth, the clean, healthy scent of him. 'And now we will carry it one step further. Say "Como".'

'Och, no . . .' Now her confusion deepened. 'You said that was . . . was for your . . .' She could not say the word; instead she substituted, 'for people who . . . who knew you really well.'

'And are you not beginning to feel that you know me, Diana? Already I begin to feel that I know you . . . Though it has only been a few days I have learned much about you—much that I like and admire.'

Diana was trying desperately to control the sensations that were flooding through her, the almost overpowering urge she had to go into his arms, to let her hands know the texture of his skin, the thick, dark hair where it curled about the nape of his neck. What on earth was happening to her?

'*You* do not dislike *me*, Diana?' he probed.

'No . . . I . . . that is . . .' She wasn't quite sure what it was she felt for him, but it most certainly didn't involve dislike.

'Perhaps you are not sure of your feelings,' he said with a startling intuitiveness. 'Perhaps I can help you to make up your mind?'

'How . . . ?' Diana began with a naïveté normally foreign to her nature. But he had her so bemused by his touch, by his proximity, that she couldn't think straight. But in any case she was not allowed to finish her question, as quite without warning his dark head blotted out the trees behind him and time and place ceased to exist as his mouth found hers.

She had never been kissed like that before. It was totally different from that other time, in the kitchen at the *palazzo*. This time it was not a fierce assault, but held a hungry yearning that in its way was no less disturbing.

The kiss grew in intensity, Giacomo's tongue probing the softness of the mouth clamped to his, and Diana let her hands have their way, learning the contours of his head, the springiness of his hair.

He kissed her eyes, her ears, her neck, the swelling curves of her breasts, making her gasp with delicious desire. His fingers ran along her spine, forcing her to arch her body towards him. Through the soft material of her dress she could feel the heat and the hardness of him.

'It is so good to hold a woman in my arms again,' he murmured against her hair, 'so good to feel sensations that I had thought dead and buried. You have brought me back to life, Diana.' He raised his head and looked into her face, into her eyes slumbrous with his lovemaking. 'Say something to me, *cara mia*. Tell me how it is with you. Are you angry with me?'

Slowly she shook her head, but she could not speak. Emotion filled her throat, choking back the words. She had never felt quite this way about a man before and she was afraid that if she spoke her feelings would spill over. Oh, it would be so easy to fall in love with him! But she was here under false pretences and it could destroy her to fall in love with Giacomo Ortoni.

'Ah, Diana, *cara mia*!' Against the sensitised skin of her neck she could feel the warm unsteadiness of his breathing.

'I am glad you are not angry. I want you as I have not wanted any woman since . . .' He broke off, then, 'I want you,' he repeated, the deep rich timbre of his voice sending shivers down her spine, and she felt her own hunger responding to its desire, 'but this is neither the time nor the place. And it is growing late.' She hadn't realised just how long they'd spent in the woods. But he kissed her once more, his mouth warm and gentle this time, and she felt his body quicken again. And perhaps his lovemaking might have been renewed if it had not been for the startling interruption.

'*Signor Aquila*!' They heard Luca's approach before they saw him. The bodyguard burst into sight through the trees, his heavy feet cracking fallen branches. As he came closer they saw it was not just exertion but alarm that contorted his features. He burst into a torrent of words so rapid and so distorted by his heavy breathing that even Diana's fluent Italian could not cope with the situation. But she had guessed that he bore bad news even before she witnessed Giacomo Ortoni's reactions.

'*Per Bacco*!' Even before Luca had finished speaking, Giacomo began to run towards the edge of the wood, the bodyguard following at a slower stumbling pace, and it took all Diana's breath and stamina to keep up with them.

So it was not until they were in the car and speeding downhill that she was able to ask, 'What's wrong? What's happened?'

'It is Maria! There has been an attempt to kidnap her.'

'How could he know that?'

'The radio,' Giacomo said tersely. 'All our vehicles are equipped with a two-way system. It is fortunate we left Luca by the cars and he heard the signal.'

Diana was longing to ask more questions, but it was

obvious that her companion needed to concentrate fully on his driving. Their speed at times around dangerous bends made her catch her breath. So it was not until they arrived at the *palazzo* that she heard the full story.

It was late evening by the time they reached the city and Florence was full of shadows and pools of darkness, lit by pretty street-lamps. Shops with single lights left burning overnight glowed from inside like toy theatres or jewel boxes. The large iron gates that guarded the building were locked as they usually were by day or night, but Ubaldo answered the bell. Ubaldo was the youngest of the three bodyguards and more slightly built. His face showed signs of having been in a fight and he was limping heavily.

Giacomo did not begin to question him until they were all inside the *palazzo*, and then Diana felt sorry for Ubaldo as he stammered out his story. But it seemed he was not to blame for the breach in security.

'Maria is safe,' Giacomo told Diana.

She had already gathered that, but then the Conte still did not know the extent of her fluency in his language.

'What happened? Ubaldo said something about Tomaso.'

Giacomo Ortoni's face was grim.

'Tomaso has proved to be a traitor. It seems he was in the pay of my enemies.'

Tomaso, Ubaldo reported, had thought himself alone in the *palazzo* with only the physiotherapist to contend with and had decided to put his long-nurtured plans into action.

'He has been in my employ for six months,' Giacomo told Diana angrily. 'He came highly recommended.'

When Tomaso had made his attempted snatch, the physiotherapist's screams had alerted Ubaldo and, though Tomaso was the most powerfully built of the three bodyguards, between them Ubaldo and the woman had managed to overpower him. The *carabinieri* had then been summoned and the venal bodyguard arrested.

Giacomo Ortoni's handsome face was still set in angry lines.

'In future I shall employ only my own people. I cannot take the risk of infiltration.'

His words made Diana cringe inwardly. What was *she* if not an infiltrator? True, she had no designs on his or Maria's safety, but she was just as guilty of deception.

'My enemies are becoming more determined,' Giacomo went on. 'I cannot afford to take any more risks. I have kept Maria near me for my own selfish reasons. She must go to Solamenza.'

Diana's heart plunged sickeningly. If the child left Florence presumably *her* services would be superfluous and she would have to leave Italy with her mission incomplete. But she did not try to deceive herself. She was less concerned about her failure to trace Julia than at the thought of leaving Giacomo Ortoni's household. It was probably the biggest mistake of her life, but she had allowed him to become far too important to her.

'Pack your things and Maria's! As quickly as possible!' Giacomo's abrupt command startled her and she looked at him uncomprehendingly. 'We leave tonight,' he said impatiently, 'now!'

'But . . .'

'No "buts", Diana, *per favore*. There is no time. News of Tomaso's arrest may precipitate further action on the part of his confederates.'

Twenty minutes later, the two limousines left the *palazzo* in convoy, Ubaldo driving the first car with Diana, Giacomo and Maria as rear-seat passengers, Luca in the second vehicle.

'Surely you could have asked for police protection?' queried Diana.

Giacomo was sardonic.

'My dear Diana, if everyone threatened by criminals were to demand protection the *carabinieri* would be stretched beyond their capabilities.' And Diana remembered the question she had been about to put to him before his kisses had driven the subject from her mind—who *were* his enemies and why?

'Who *are* these people? Doesn't most of the organised crime in this country have its roots in the activities of the Mafia? But why should the Mafia be interested in *you*?' And with a cold thrill of fear, 'You're . . . you're not one of them, are you?'

His laugh held genuine amusement.

'You forget—*my* branch of the family is "respectable". But no, the Mafia are not involved. Do not concern your pretty head over such matters, Diana. They are for men to deal with.' Female equality obviously wasn't rife in southern Italy, Diana thought wryly. '*Your* task is to go on caring for Maria.'

'How long shall we have to stay at Solamenza?'

'*Chi lo sa*? Who knows? Weeks, months—a year perhaps. Until certain affairs have been concluded and I am sure it is safe for you and Maria to return to Florence.'

Diana was aghast. She was already into the first of her two weeks' unpaid leave. There was no way she could stay in Italy beyond that period. She struggled for words.

'When . . . when I applied for this job I had no idea there would be danger involved.' She swallowed. She wasn't really a coward and she was about to sink very low in Giacomo Ortoni's estimation, but she had no other choice. 'I . . . I'm afraid I shall have to hand in my notice. I'll . . .

I'll stay for another week, until you can make alternative arrangements. But then . . .'

'Diana!' he interrupted her, his voice cold and stern. 'You do not seem to understand. What threatens me threatens all around me. Once we reach Solamenza, no one leaves until I say so!'

CHAPTER FOUR

'HAVE no fear!' At her little gasp of dismay Giacomo's voice gentled and his hand clasped her knee. His touch was probably meant to be reassuring, but it made her tremble. 'I will not let any harm come to you, *cara mia*. At Solamenza you will be protected against all danger.'

Physical danger maybe, Diana thought, but there was an even greater peril. Incarceration with Giacomo in his mountain retreat could only increase the opportunities for intimacy, and she knew she was already more than half in love with him.

'Try to sleep now,' Giacomo advised her, and his arm went around her, further disturbing her composure. 'We have a long drive ahead of us.'

She thought it would be impossible, but despite the agitation caused by his proximity she did sleep, and woke just as dawn was breaking over the wild mountainous land of the Abruzzi. Maria, she noticed, was still soundly asleep.

'Not much further now,' said Giacomo when Diana stirred and moved stiffly out of his embrace to look around her.

'Goodness, it's a bit bleak, isn't it?'

And the mountains grew bleaker with every mile. The land was unnaturally contorted and twisted. Rocks which appeared to have been thrown down from the mountain tops lay scattered everywhere in the narrow valleys.

The road was an angry serpent writhing and twisting,

with rock precipices towering on one side and a sheer drop on the other. Their vehicle lurched around a corner, and for a moment appeared to hang suspended over a precipitous drop. Diana was thrown hard against the Conte's chest. For an instant she lay there, hearing the pounding of his heart.

'You are nervous?' Giacomo enquired as Diana drew in a sharp breath.

'A . . . a little,' she confessed, glad of this excuse for the way she was trembling.

But it was his proximity that had caused her reaction, though she was finding motoring in this mountainous country a strain on the nerves. But it was more than compensated for by the excitement of being on the threshold of new scenes, new experiences. For the moment she had forgotten her invidious position in the Conte's household and the difficulties she might experience in leaving Solamenza.

'I forget others are not accustomed to such scenes,' Giacomo went on. 'We Abruzzi are a hardy race. We have to be to live in these remote mountain villages.'

In the silence that followed Diana was embarrassingly aware that her stomach was rumbling, and Giacomo must have heard it too.

'Are you hungry?' he asked.

'Mmm, ravenous!' she confessed.

And so, just before the road entered a narrow pass, they stopped at a wayside *albergo* for breakfast.

To Diana's surprise the Conte chose to sit apart with her, leaving the bodyguards to cope with his daughter's needs. As they ate he spoke in low earnest tones to her.

'I have to apologise to you for the arbitrary manner in which I carried you off from Florence. But believe me, it was necessary.' And as Diana, despite her forebodings, felt bound to murmur a polite disclaimer, 'But I admit I am glad of this chance to show you the place I look upon above all others as my home. I want you to like Solamenza, Diana.'

'I'm sure I shall,' she said, and not altogether from a sense of politeness.

'When I was first married I made my home there all year round and the *palazzo* stood empty except when affairs necessitated my presence in Florence. But . . . circumstances gave me a distaste for the castle. For the past three years I have lived at the *palazzo*.' It surely couldn't be coincidental that his wife had died three years previously, Diana mused with a little painful tug of her heartstrings. 'But it may be, now, that I shall return permanently to Solamenza.'

'You'd prefer that?'

'It is my home,' he said simply.

After breakfast they drove on through the pass. Ahead, stretched across the sky, was a shining band of white.

'The mountains of the Gran Sasso d'Italia,' Giacomo explained.

These, the highest mountains in the Apennines, were still covered in snow. And Diana shivered as the road through the pass grew higher and the air came cold and crisp from the snowfields.

'You are cold!' Giacomo ordered Luca to step up the vehicle's heating system and drew her back into the circle of his arm. He tucked a travelling rug securely about her, and as he did so she thought she felt his lips brush her blonde curls, but she could not be certain.

The road descended a little now and the barren mountains gave way to slopes covered in yellow broom. Maria was wide awake after her breakfast and her stubborn silence seemed even stranger in these circumstances. Any other child would have been full of questions and comments on their journey, Diana thought. Nevertheless she addressed the child as though the situation were normal.

'Your father tells me we are nearly there. But I expect you know this road very well.'

When, as expected, Maria did not answer, Giacomo pointed ahead of them where the road swooped upwards once more to the crest of a mountain. The silhouetted shape of buildings could be seen standing above a gorge and clinging to vertiginous ledges.

'Havers! It looks like a castle!' Diana exclaimed, her blue eyes wide with amazement.

'Probably because it *is* a castle,' Giacomo told her with a smile. 'It was built in the eleventh century by Rainulf Ortoni.'

'And it's still standing!' she marvelled.

'Many people have attempted to overthrow it, including Tancred's descendants, but the Castle of Solamenza was built to last. Because of its position it has been likened to an eagle's eyrie, and the Counts of Solamenza have always been nicknamed . . .'

'*L'Aquila*,' Diana finished for him. 'The Eagle of Solamenza.'

'You have heard the expression?'

'From Tomaso and . . .'

'You became very friendly, it seems, with Tomaso!' He was frowning with displeasure.

'I *was* going to say Luca and Ubaldo use it too,' she told him, and his face cleared.

'Of course—forgive me. It is a bad thing when I become suspicious even of my friends. But treachery—from friend or foe—is something I could never forgive.' Diana felt the sudden warmth in her cheeks and beneath the travelling rug she groped for her lucky charm.

Now they were ascending the mountain via a series of bloodcurdling hairpin bends, the road only just wide enough for the large limousine.

Once, Giacomo told Diana, the town of Solamenza had only been approachable by way of a mule track. But in comparatively recent times the road had been cut into the mountain, winding and twisting through the magnificent scenery. The way was marked at intervals with lines of tall striped posts.

'It is subject to snowdrifts in winter,' he explained. 'One can be cut off for months.' And Diana offered up a silent prayer of thanks that it was spring. For somehow, in less than two weeks, she had to persuade the Conte to allow her to leave Solamenza.

They were on the far side of the mountain now and she could see houses rising in terraces towards the hexagonal castle with its six machicolated towers.

It was only possible to drive as far as the embattled gateway of the town.

'When my ancestor built and fortified Solamenza,' Giacomo told her, 'he could not foresee the advent of cars.'

With one of the bodyguards pushing Maria's wheelchair, they walked, carrying their luggage, through the steep, narrow cobbled lanes that ran beneath Arabic-looking arches. Medieval and Renaissance buildings stood everywhere. Some had delightful stone window frames, others had balconies. Picturesque flights of steps led to some houses.

The castle itself had a watchful, almost forbidding air to it as though a hundred brooding secrets dwelt behind its dusky façade, and Diana was astonished when Giacomo actually led the way right up to its old gold and brown walls.

'You don't actually live in the castle, do you?' she asked.

'Of course.' He smiled. 'Do not look so alarmed. I think you will be pleasantly surprised.'

There was no moat and no drawbridge, Diana noticed. Instead, in answer to the Conte's summons an elderly man opened a small picket gate and their party filed through on to the grooved paving stones of a large courtyard.

Once inside, the architecture of the castle was more apparent—an exercise in hexagons carried out on two storeys. A hexagonal courtyard surrounded by six rooms was repeated exactly on the floor above. There was a certain degree of modernisation, Diana was to discover later, for the six hexagonal towers, despite their stone spiral staircases, also contained bathrooms.

From outside, the castle with its towers lit by arrow slits might have looked antiquated and forbidding. Inside it had the luxury and elegance of a Renaissance palace.

The arrival of the Conte and his daughter was a signal for great excitement. Within moments of their arrival they were surrounded by a noisy gesticulating group of people, family and servants alike, Diana later discovered. Italians when excited always sounded as though they were on the verge of fisticuffs. But a few words from Giacomo in a raised voice and the crowd magically dispersed except for an elderly woman clad in rusty black whom Giacomo introduced as the housekeeper.

'Assunta,' he addressed the woman in Italian, 'show Signorina Watt to the room opposite Maria's.'

At once the housekeeper broke into a spate of words too rapid even for Diana to follow, but it was obviously a protest, and when Giacomo bade her sharply to be quiet and do as she was told Assunta submitted, but with a very bad grace. The elderly woman continued to mutter under her breath as she led the way up a winding flight of stairs. Luca followed behind, carrying Maria in his arms, Ubaldo following behind with the folded wheelchair.

Luca carried the child into her room and Assunta, with an outraged sniff, threw open a door on the opposite side of the landing.

'What was all the blethering about?' Diana asked Maria when the housekeeper and the bodyguards had left them alone in the child's room.

'Assunta disapproves of my father giving you that room. It has not been used for three years.' And Diana guessed what was coming next before the words were out. 'It was my mother's room.'

'Oh, dear!' Diana was dismayed. 'Do . . . do *you* mind me using it, Maria?'

The child considered for a moment, her auburn head on one side, her pale, heart-shaped face grave. Then she smiled.

'No. I like you. I would have minded if it had been one of the others.'

'Have there been many other girls looking after you?'

'Five or six—I lost count. But,' an impish grin, 'I soon got rid of them.'

'Why didn't you like *them*?'

'They were not interested in *me*,' said Maria with simple matter-of-factness and with an insight startling for her age. 'They were only interested in my father.' She scowled suddenly. 'They would not have been if they had known what I know about him.'

Diana was in a dilemma. She longed for the child to be

more explicit, and yet she couldn't bring herself to ask questions. It was her business here to find out all she could about Giacomo Ortoni, and yet it seemed despicable to make use of his small daughter, especially when the rift between father and daughter was already so wide. She hesitated, and the moment was lost, for Maria was propelling her chair towards the door.

'Come and see your room,' she invited.

'All right,' Diana agreed, then as the chair preceded her, 'Remind me to ask someone to oil that chair. One of the wheels is squeaking abominably.'

On the threshold of Sandra Ortoni's room, Diana drew in her breath. The room was a boudoir in the true romantic style—pink carpets and curtains, walls washed grey-white, the ceiling painted with pink roses and birds. Despite the fact that it had stood empty for three years its occupant might only have left it for a moment. It was spotlessly clean, fresh and fragrantly perfumed. Toiletries and silver-backed hairbrushes stood on the dressing-table flanking an ornately framed photograph of Giacomo Ortoni. A négligé edged with swansdown still lay across a chair, a matching pair of slippers beneath it.

'It's almost like a shrine,' said Diana, unaware that she was speaking her thoughts aloud. 'He must have loved her very much.'

'He did not!' Maria's words held a harshness that should never have been present in a child's voice.

Diana was shocked, and with her eyes intent on the child's contorted face she did not see the bedroom door open.

'But someone has kept this room so beautifully.'

'That will be Assunta,' Maria said. 'She adored my mother—and so did I.'

'*Per carita!*'

Startled, Diana and Maria turned to see Giacomo Ortoni standing in the doorway, his handsome face irradiated by a smile. But as her father advanced towards her the child's mouth set into its usual stubborn lines.

Giacomo crouched down by the wheelchair, his astounding green eyes, alight with love, on a level with his daughter's. He put a hand on her slight shoulder.

'Maria, *bambina mia*, you have found your voice!' He waited expectantly, but with a gesture of rejection the child steered herself away from him, the chair squeaking its way to the other side of the room where she stared resolutely out of the window.

Giacomo stood up and Diana's heart ached for the hurt in his face. Her large, widely spaced eyes filled with compassion. Involuntarily she made a move towards him, hand outstretched. But he drew back, his features immediately drawn into harsh planes of inscrutability.

'When you have finished your unpacking please come down to the *salone* and meet my family.' He swung round on his heel and left the room, and Diana knew a sense of rejection that equalled his own.

'Maria!' she turned to the child in gentle reproach. 'I wish I knew why you treat your poor father like that. He loves you.'

'He did not love my mother, that is why.'

'Oh, Maria, I'm sure you're wrong. He . . .'

'I do not want to talk about it,' the child interrupted rudely. It was the first time she had spoken to Diana in such a tone since their first meeting. Suspiciously, 'Why are you standing up for him?'

'I'm not. I . . .'

'You had better hurry up and do as he says. Go and meet

his family.'

'Maria,' Diana was gentle with her despite the rudeness, 'they *are* your family too. You can't deny it however much you try.'

'But I can dis . . . dis . . .' The child sought for the correct English word. 'I can disown them if I like. They are on *his* side. Otherwise he would not be able to get away with what he did.'

Diana knew of the strong loyalties of Italian families; they might almost have coined the phrase 'one for all and all for one'. It was the sense of oneness that had led to so many feuds down the centuries. But for heaven's sake, what crime of Giacomo Ortoni's were his family conniving to hide?

Her heart felt heavy as she descended the main staircase and went in search of the *salone*. But this was ridiculous, she upbraided herself. She had come to Italy, her brain rife with her aunt's suspicions of the Conte Ortoni. She ought to be glad that she seemed to be getting closer to proof of his misdeeds. Instead she found herself hoping desperately that Maria's words pointed only to a childish exaggeration or some imagined wrong.

On a lower floor she encountered Assunta and politely enquired the way to the *salone*. But in place of an answer she received only a dark glance accompanied by an odd gesture of the hand, the woman's first and fourth fingers pointing to the earth.

Strange. Diana knew very well that none of the principal rooms would be on the ground floor.

Finally it was the sound of voices that guided her to her target, a large apartment with a floor of soft red tiles, oiled and polished like glass. The room, at first glance, seemed to be full of people all apparently talking at once, and she paused, irresolute, on the threshold.

But Giacomo's sharp eyes had observed her. He seemed to have shaken off his dour mood and he greeted her with one of the smiles that had the power to weaken her knees.

'Diana, *avanti*! Let me introduce you to my aunts and uncles and my brother.' The crowd resolved itself into five elderly people and a younger man, perhaps in his mid-twenties. She moved from one to the other, shaking hands, trying to fix their names in her head.

Bonifacio and Biella, Fabrizio and Faustina were twins. Fabrizio and his sister Faustina, tall, lean Ortonis, were non-identical. But the plump Bonifacio and *his* twin sister Biella were so alike that it was comical. Celestina Ortoni was the wife of yet another uncle, Sergio, at present in Rome, Diana gathered.

'And *mio fratello*, Stefano,' Giacomo introduced.

Stefano Ortoni was nothing like his elder brother. Where Giacomo was tall with a hard muscular body, Stefano ran to plumpness, his handshake was soft and a little moist. His mouth and chin were weak; his hair was of a paler shade and already thinning. Only the green eyes were the same, but they hadn't the directness of Giacomo's.

'S-Signorina W-Watt!' He spoke with a slight stammer. In fact his whole manner was indicative of a nervous man.

'I hope you'll all call me Diana,' she suggested. 'Gi . . . the Conte does.' Suddenly she was shy of using his name in front of his family. The older generation in particular might find it presumptuous.

It was evening when Giacomo tore Diana away from his family and took her on a tour of the castle. During the afternoon the sun had dispersed the mountain mists and it was still quite warm, warm enough for them to shed their sweaters.

The castle was very typical of its kind, Diana thought,

with its gargoyles, steeply pitched roofs and even a dungeon.

'Encountered *en masse*, I am afraid my family must seem rather daunting?' said Giacomo.

'A wee bit,' she admitted. But on the whole, she decided, she liked Giacomo Ortoni's family. Celestina had been scrupulously polite. Fabrizio and Faustina were perhaps a little stiff in their manner, but the other pair of twins were warm and friendly, while Stefano seemed almost pathetically eager to please. And Giacomo confirmed her thoughts.

'But without exception they all liked you,' Giacomo assured her.

'I'm glad. I don't think your housekeeper does, though.'

'Ah!' A fleeting expression of pain crossed his face. 'She was very devoted to Sandra. She sees every other woman who comes here as a threat to her memory.' And then, his words giving Diana a pang, 'I have told her time and again that this is not so. Assunta may disapprove,' he went on, 'but she will treat you with courtesy. She knows that to do otherwise would incur my displeasure.'

'What does this mean?' Diana demonstrated for him the odd sign the housekeeper had made.

Giacomo looked annoyed.

'Assunta?' he asked, and as she nodded, 'It is the sign of the horns, the sign against the evil eye.'

'She surely doesn't believe . . .?'

'It may have something to do with the charm you wear about your neck—a black cat. Cats are traditionally associated with witchcraft.' And as Diana made a sound of incredulity, 'You must remember civilisation has been slow in coming to these mountain villages. It takes more than modern transport and television to change the mentality of centuries. Some of the old ones still believe in omens, in witches and werewolves, and many of them still wear amulets to ward off the evil eye. Surely you of all people must sympathise?' He laughed a little ruefully and pulled a keyring from his pocket from which dangled a small red hand, the fingers making the familiar gesture. 'And even I, though I am not superstitious, subscribe to tradition.'

'But why should Assunta take *me* for a witch?' Diana asked indignantly. They had just ascended a steep spiral staircase which brought them out on to the battlements just below the humped tiles of the roof, russet, yellow ochre and green in the evening sunlight. She turned abruptly to confront him with her question. Because he was still a step or two behind her their faces were on a level and she looked straight into the eyes which somehow always compelled her gaze. They were quizzical now.

'Perhaps,' he said lightly, 'she thinks you have bewitched me.' There was a long pregnant silence during which Diana found she was holding her breath. Then, more seriously, he went on, 'You see, no other woman has ever been permitted to use that room.'

'Then why me?' she asked bluntly. She turned away and crossed to the battlements, staring down over the confused tiled roofs of the town below.

Giacomo moved to stand beside her, so close that the fine hairs on his bare forearm brushed hers, and Diana felt the muscles of her abdomen clench tightly against the sensual little thrill.

'Perhaps,' he said soberly, 'because it is time to put such memories away where they belong—in the past.'

'But you said you'd assured Assunta . . .'

'Naturally I shall not forget Sandra. What I meant when I made that promise was that my first wife will always have her place in my memory. But another may also have *her* place.'

'I see,' Diana said dully. It sounded as if he was getting really serious about his idea of remarrying. And she had to force herself to sound enthusiastic as he asked, 'And what do you think of my home, now that you have seen it?'

'It's certainly unusual.'

'To you, perhaps,' he agreed. 'And it is true there are not many such in habitable condition. But the ruins of Norman castles still crown a hundred hilltops. This one has been made as comfortable as all modern conveniences can make it.' And, as she did not reply, 'But perhaps you find it too primitive, the surroundings too wild and uncivilised?'

'No, it's bonnie.'

And it was, on that May evening. The dying sun was like gold that poured down over everything. Goats, looking like toy farmyard animals, wandered the steep tracks on the slopes of the mountain, grazing the sparse tufts of grass. The air was filled with the smell of wild thyme and other herbs. Far below them a lake reflected the luminous snowcaps of other surrounding mountains.

'Could *you* live here?' Giacomo asked softly.

Even though her thoughts had been running on those lines, Diana was unprepared for the sudden challenge.

'I . . . I don't really know.' But she did. Then with an attempt at flippancy, 'It's always difficult to answer questions that are purely academic.'

'And if it were not merely academic?'

She dared not look at him but continued to stare out over the rugged countryside.

'I don't quite . . .' she began.

'Suppose I were to ask you to stay here—always?'

Diana had to swallow before she could answer, because he

could not mean . . .

'Maria won't always need a companion. She'll grow up and . . .'

'And what of me? Shall I not need a companion?'

Wilfully she chose to misunderstand, but only because she dared not do otherwise.

'Your castle seems pretty full to me already—I shouldn't think you ever go short of company. I assume all those uncles and aunts *do* live here?'

'They do, but . . .' he brushed the subject aside, 'it was not that kind of companionship to which I referred. I think you know that, Diana.' He put his hands on her shoulders and forced her to turn and look at him.

'I . . . I'm not a mind-reader.' But colour scorched her face and her blue eyes were enormous.

'You don't have to be. Don't my physical reactions to you tell you anything?' And without waiting for an answer he pressed her hard against him, forcing her awareness of a stirring masculine desire that surged hard and strong against her abdomen.

'Como,' she protested, 'please . . . I . . .'

'Ah, I was beginning to think you had forgotten my name!' Retaining his tight hold of her, he pressed gently on her chin, just below her lower lip, causing her mouth to open slightly, and as it did so his tongue probed her mouth's inner warm, the sensation making her tremble violently. 'I told you once before that I wanted you, Diana, but the place and the time were not right and we were interrupted. Here at Solamenza there will be plenty of time and—I hope—no interruptions.'

Her head was swimming, her heart beating frantically, and she wanted nothing more than to have him go on talking this way, caressing her the way he was caressing her.

But her senses were not totally swamped by his sexuality. This was the man who had been involved with Julia. She fought to free herself. But he would not release her and his tone was a little rueful as he said, 'I think I am falling in love with you, Diana.'

'Oh, no! I mean . . . you . . . you can't be!'

'Why not?' with husky tenderness.

'It . . . it's just physical,' she said desperately. She was trying to convince herself as much as him. 'It must be. You said yourself you're just beginning to come to terms with the death of your wife. You're beginning to want . . .'

'*You*, Diana, as I told you. I do not feel this way about any other woman.'

'Perhaps because you haven't encountered many lately. I mean, you wouldn't have much chance, would you, always surrounded by bodyguards?' She summoned a laugh, but it rang false even to her own ears.

He held her a little away from him, but not so far that she could not still sense his urgent needs. His green eyes searched her face.

'Why are you trying so earnestly to dissuade me?' he asked. 'Do you not wish to be loved and wanted?' Oh, if he only knew! But it was as well he did not.

'It . . . it's just that I can't believe anyone can fall in love so quickly.' Her voice was low and earnest, her accent very pronounced. 'It's only a few days since you disliked me, thought I was . . . And we still hardly know each other.'

'You do not actively dislike me?'

'N-no, but . . .'

'Then all that is needed,' he said with palpable satisfaction, 'is for us to get to know each other better? You need more time? Is that not it?'

Diana grasped at the excuse.

'Aye, that's it. But . . . but there's still no guarantee that . . .'

'No?' There was an almost arrogant note in his voice. 'I think—I hope—that you underestimate me, Diana. I think *I* can make a guarantee—to teach you to love me. And why should the lesson not start now?'

Diana had been kissed by several men before she had ever met Giacomo Ortoni. But never once had she experienced the mind-reeling impact that his kisses seemed to have on her. They reached down deep inside her to her most vulnerable core. Now she found herself reacting to him with an almost pagan response that shocked her.

When Giacomo lifted his head she couldn't meet his eyes, but fixed her gaze somewhere in the centre of his chest, which rose and fell in a most alarming way, indicating the kiss's effect on him.

'*Cara mia,*' he breathed, 'that was a most promising beginning!' As he spoke he bent towards her again. His mouth drained all her remaining will to resist as he parted her lips, tasting their inner sweetness.

Her arms crept up about his neck, and now their bodies could not be close enough for her as she shuddered under his touch, his hands shaping and caressing her. And she groaned in protest when he tore his mouth from hers and put her away from him.

'Next time,' he said, 'we will take more care in choosing the place.' And she realised his sharp ears had picked up a faint sound that had been lost to her in the thudding of her pulses. 'What is it, Assunta?' he greeted the housekeeper.

There was outrage in every taut line of her angular body. Even the rustle of her black dress expressed Assunta's disapproval.

'The uncles and aunts are ready to eat.' And then she

went into what Diana recognised as a repeat performance of her earlier diatribe.

She had expected a fiercer reaction from Giacomo, but he was gentle with the old woman. An arm about her shoulders, he remonstrated with her, but without rancour. He turned to Diana.

'I am sorry, I had not realised it had grown so late. You will wish time to change. I will have Assunta delay the meal for twenty minutes. Will that be long enough?'

It was long enough to dress for dinner. It certainly wasn't long enough for any prolonged heart-searching or to steady her inner turmoil.

There was no time to shower. Diana washed quickly in the old-fashioned bedroom ewer and slipped into fresh undies. She hesitated for a moment over her choice of dress, knowing that her irresolution was due to a wish to look attractive in Giacomo's eyes, and for that reason deliberately she chose a black sheath dress, the least favourite of her outfits, one that she had never been quite certain suited her. Those moments up on the battlement had been moments of madness during which she had almost begun to believe in the possibility of a relationship between herself and Giacomo Ortoni. Sane again now, she knew it was necessary to nip that blossoming attraction in the bud before it was too late. If it were not already too late!

The Ortonis dined in befitting style. Nothing primitive or uncivilised about the array of silver and pure white napery, about the delectable mouth-watering food, course after course of it.

Diana was relieved that she did not have to sit next to Giacomo. But then, since she was still only an *au pair* girl in the sight of his family, it would not have been considered suitable. She was placed at the far end of the table, with Zia

Biella on one side and Stefano on the other. Maria was not considered old enough to dine with the family.

Stefano's English was not as fluent as that of his older brother and Diana still did not wish to betray her own excellent Italian. Nevertheless they managed to communicate.

'You are very d-different from the other g-girls who have been hired to look after Maria.'

'In what way?' Diana asked curiously.

Head on one side, he considered her.

'Firstly I think it is that you have a g-greater maturity. Secondly I think it is perhaps that you c-come from a better family. The others were . . . I think the English word is "c-common"? Their behaviour towards my brother left much to be desired.'

'Maria said much the same,' Diana said without thinking, and at once Stefano was alert. She thought she even sensed a certain unease in him.

'You have managed to g-get Maria to talk to you? Does Como know of this?'

'Yes,' Diana said ruefully, 'and I'm afraid he's rather hurt because she won't speak to *him*.'

To her surprise Stefano waved that aside.

'What d-does Maria say to you?'

'Oh, the kind of things wee girls normally talk about—books, clothes. She is very interested in England.'

'But she has spoken about these other g-girls?'

'Not in detail, only to say she didn't like any of them.'

'I see.' Did Stefano breathe a sigh of relief? Was this weak-featured young man with his diffident manner perhaps a better target for her curiosity? Could *he* be a lead to Julia?

'Did you expect her to have said something in particular?'

she asked.

'No, of course not.' He was sharp, his stammer vanishing, and shortly afterwards he made an excuse to turn towards Faustina, his other neighbour, and eagerly Biella claimed Diana's attention.

'I heard you tell Stefano that Maria talks to you. How have you worked this miracle?'

Diana smiled as she remembered her tactics.

'By pretending I didn't *want* her to talk to me.'

Biella was obviously impressed.

'Now why did no one else ever think of that? But then Stefano is right—you are much more intelligent than those other girls.' Evidently Biella had sharp ears. 'You know the *medicos* say there is nothing wrong with Maria?'

'Aye, and they were obviously right when it comes to her speech. But I don't think she's faking not being able to walk.'

Biella nodded her mouse-nest heap of hair.

'I agree. And it is certain the child had a nasty fall, only days after her mother died.'

Diana had no doubt Biella would have said more, but it seemed the Ortinis were sticklers for tradition in all its forms, and Faustina, the older sister, gave the signal for the ladies to leave the table. When they adjourned to the *salone* the conversation became general, the ladies asking Diana, not about England as she would have expected, but about Florence and Rome.

'We have not left Solamenza in nearly two years,' grumbled Faustina. 'It is a long time. There will have been changes in the cities.'

'It is for our own good,' Celestina put in quietly. Her manner towards the older woman was almost deferential. Then, with greater emphasis, 'It is also for Sergio's sake.'

She turned to Diana. 'Sergio holds an important position in the government,' she said with evident pride. 'For two years he has been fighting for a most important reform. But he has many enemies who will try anything to discredit him—even to the extent of kidnapping members of his family in order to bring pressure to bear on him, to force him to abandon his policies.'

'I still think Giacomo exaggerates the dangers,' Faustina put in. 'I can see no earthly reason why we should remain here indefinitely. Surely we would be safe enough at the family *palazzo* in Firenze?'

From this Diana gathered the Conte had not told them about the attempted kidnapping of Maria in Florence. No doubt he wished to spare his elderly relatives anxiety. From their age it was evident that two generations separated them from their nephew, making them great-uncles and aunts.

This was so, Biella revealed as the conversation continued.

'And he is *un buon uomo*—a good man—our Como, to give a home to us all.' And the other two elderly women nodded. Apparently neither set of twins had ever married. Somehow the years had gone by and now none of them could face the upheaval of moving from their childhood home. 'But our younger brother Sergio has lived in the world,' Biella told Diana proudly. 'But though he is so important in the Government he married Celestina here, his sweetheart from his home town. And when he retires he will also return here to live.'

'How did Sandra—the Conte's wife—feel about living with so many of her husband's relations?' Diana asked.

Biella beamed.

'She loved us and we loved her.' Again the other two nodded. Biella, who seemed to have elected herself spokeswoman, sighed heavily. '*Dio mio*, but there will never be another one like Sandra!'

Diana's stomach churned.

'You don't think your great-nephew will ever marry again?'

There was an immediate chorus of 'no's'.

'Oh, no,' Biella said again with great confidence. 'There will be women, of course—he is a man. But he will never put anyone in Sandra's place.'

Sagely Faustina and Celestina nodded.

Diana supposed she ought to have been relieved by this general consensus of opinion, this almost certain confirmation that Giacomo Ortoni was not serious in his attentions to her. In actual fact she felt decidedly depressed. Not only was it very lowering to realise that in all probability what he was after was just an affair; it was also dispiriting to discover how much she wanted his expressed affection to stand for something more genuine and permanent.

The men arrived, breaking up the cosy little circle of confidantes, the conversation turned towards less intimate topics and soon, to Diana's relief, it was time for bed. It had been a long day, beginning from that awakening in the car to this moment. And so much seemed to have been crammed into the intervening hours, not least a whole host of conflicting emotions.

She found Maria still awake when she went in to say goodnight.

'You should be asleep, lassie,' Diana chided gently, but the child shook her head.

'I cannot sleep. There is too much to think about.'

Nevertheless Diana stayed with the little girl until her eyes drooped and she slept.

Though she was tired, Diana wasn't sure she would be able to relax. Like Maria, she felt there were too many things to think about. In moments of tension she usually found a bath the best remedy.

Fluffy towels were hung on a rail at the foot of her bed, but, she realised, she had no idea where the bathroom was situated. Then she spotted a panelled door she had not noticed before, it was so skilfully decorated to look one with the wall.

Of course, she thought thankfully—an en-suite bathroom. The castle had been extensively modernised. The present generation of Ortonis would want their creature comforts.

She undressed quickly, wrapped one of the towels about her, flung open the panelled door and stepped inside. The next moment she was recoiling with alarm. This was no bathroom. She had passed through a communicating door into another bedroom.

Worse, it was not just any room, but Giacomo's. And he was there, clad only in a silky robe that barely skimmed his muscular thighs.

'Och I . . . I'm sorry,' stammered Diana, her arms wrapped protectively about her towel-clad body, 'I . . . I thought . . .'

'Do not apologise!' he said warmly, and before she could retreat he moved swiftly towards her. 'Had you not made the first move I would have come in search of you.'

'But I didn't . . . You don't understand . . . I . . .'

'Have no fear. There will be no interruptions here, Diana, *cara mia*. At last we have found the right place and the right time.'

Before she could protest further he had swept her into his arms against his already hardening body and his mouth covered hers, brooking no denial, and it was not long before, all resistance overcome, her lips parted beneath his.

Diana shuddered as his hands stroked her bare shoulders, the sensation of his warm flesh on hers making her delirious with pleasure. His fingers discovered the curve of her breast and found their way inside the towel's folds to caress and tantalise.

His kiss intensified, becoming an exploration of her mouth that made her dizzy. Desire flooded her and she felt her tormented nipples hardening against his hands.

His questing mouth traced the tender skin of her neck. He nibbled sensuously, sending shockwaves of pleasure through her quivering form. Her bemused mind registered that he had showered recently, for his clean male scent engulfed her, completing the enslavement of her senses.

She wanted to touch him too, and she slid her hands beneath the revers of his robe, heard his sudden indrawn breath and the slight shudder that went through him as she pressed her lips against the warm column of his throat. Vaguely, she was aware that the bathtowel was giving up its precarious protection.

Giacomo was aware of it too, and his grasp of her tightened as she snatched the towel back into place. She could feel the heated pressure of his thighs through the thin silky material of his robe. His hands slid down her naked back and cupped her buttocks, each caress making her long feverishly for a greater intimacy with his body.

An ache was building up within her and she moaned as his hands moved with increasing urgency and she arched against him.

'I am going to make love to you, Diana,' he muttered throatily against the delicate rim of her ear. 'And when it is all over you will never want to leave me . . . never.'

CHAPTER FIVE

GIACOMO lifted his head and looked down into Diana's bedazzled eyes, and at that moment he could have made her his and she would not have done anything to stop him. But then his gaze shifted past hers, his passion-glazed eyes widened and hardened and he gave a hoarse exclamation of annoyance. In the heat of the moment he spoke in his own language, but his meaning was unmistakable.

'*Get out*!'

For a wild instant Diana thought he was speaking to her, but then she heard a familiar squeaking sound and turned her head to see the rear view of Maria's wheelchair as the child beat a hasty retreat.

Diana wrenched herself free, thanking her lucky stars that she had readjusted the towel, and made to follow the child, but Giacomo pulled her back.

'Como, please,' she protested, 'I must go to her and explain . . .'

He swore lustily.

'*Sacramento*! You do not owe Maria any explanation.'

'But I do. I don't want to lose the wee lassie's trust. I don't want her to think I'm like . . .'

'Like whom?' he interrupted sharply, and she looked at him in surprise.

'Surely you know?'

'No,' grimly, 'I do not. What are you talking about?'

'I don't want Maria to think I'm like the other girls you

102

employed to look after her.' Curiously, 'What on earth did you think I was going to say?'

He waved that aside impatiently.

'It does not matter. What is it that Maria is not to think about you?'

The colour ran up in her cheeks, but she answered him truthfully.

'That I'm more interested in chasing you than in looking after her.'

His brow cleared.

'Ah, yes. Some of them were anxious to become the wife of a *conte*, I think. They would not know that the title carries no great prestige these days.' With obvious reluctance he released her. 'Go to Maria, then. And,' throatily, 'come back here to me afterwards.'

But with her sanity restored by the interruption, Diana had no intention of doing anything of the kind. Passing through her own room, she closed the communicating door and softly turned the key in the lock before going in search of Maria.

The child's door was locked too when Diana tried it.

'Maria! Maria, let me in. I must talk to you.'

Silence.

'Maria! Please!'

But though she stood for a long while calling the child's name, repeating her request to be let in, there was no response. At last, disconsolately, Diana returned to her own room.

Giacomo was waiting for her, sitting on the edge of her bed, and the communicating door had been thrown wide open again. His green eyes glittered angrily.

'What game is this you are playing with me, Diana? Why did you lock the door?'

'Because I can't take up where we left off just like that . . . not when Maria . . . And anyway . . .' he might as well know the truth, 'I only came into your room in the first place because I thought it was a bathroom.'

'You thought . . .?' He stared at her for a long time and his face worked strangely.

She was expecting an explosion of anger, but the outburst when it came was one of amusement. Thank goodness! His sense of humour had asserted itself. A relieved Diana felt her own mouth twitch. But then, to her dismay, instead of joining in his laughter she felt the tears begin to trickle down her cheeks.

His mirth was stilled instantly.

'Diana?' He stood up and came towards her. 'What is it, *cara mia*?'

'N-nothing—I'm all right. Leave me alone.' She waved aside his outstretched arms. 'Please, Como, just go away.'

'Not until you tell me what is upsetting you. Is it Maria? Is it I? I could have sworn you were happy in my arms.'

'But it wouldn't have ended there, would it?' she hiccupped. 'Next thing I'd have found myself in your bed. And I'm not like that, Como. I won't have an affair with you.'

'Who is talking about an affair?' Suddenly he was all stiff pride. 'The Ortonis have never gone in for clandestine affairs. We court only the women we intend to marry.'

'T-to *marry*?' It came out on an undignified squeak.

'But of course. Did I not tell you I was falling in love with you?'

'Aye, but . . . but I didn't think you meant . . . and Zia Biella said . . .' Diana realised she was becoming incoherent. She took a deep steadying breath. 'Your aunts all seemed to think that you were too much in love with your first wife ever to marry again. So I thought . . .'

'So you thought I would insult you . . . a guest in my home . . . by taking you to my bed to satisfy some animal urge!' He was outraged. 'I had thought you knew me better than that.'

'That's the trouble!' Her anger flared in answer to his own, drying her tears. But she was angry now with herself rather than with him. 'I don't know you at all—not enough to get involved in this way. And—' thinking of her mission to find Julia—'I only have *your* word for the kind of man you are.'

'What exactly do you mean by that?' The question came from between the white clenched teeth.

'I mean that we come from two totally different worlds, culturally speaking. There are so many differences in our upbringing. I don't know how you feel about . . . about certain things . . .' She didn't like to put it into actual words. For despite his denial that he indulged in affairs, she couldn't help thinking about what Biella had said—that there were women in his life. After all, he was a young virile man—and only too human.

'There is something in your life you are reluctant—perhaps ashamed—to tell me?' Giacomo demanded.

'Och, no!' she cried indignantly. Then she flushed, remembering her present masquerade. 'At least, not the sort of thing *you* mean. But there you are, you see, you've only got my word for it. And the same goes for you. How do *I* know what *you've* done in the past?'

He was gravely offended now. She could tell by the set of his lips, the twin vertical lines between his flashing eyes.

'When one loves,' he said, 'there is trust—trust for the *future*. The years before you met me are the past and I shall not question you about them.' Then the anger which had held him rigid faded and his shoulders slumped, wearily she thought. 'I love you, Diana. But it seems *you* do not love *me*?'

But she did. Emotion engulfed her, longing mingled with despair. Inwardly she cursed the shadow of Julia that formed a barrier between them. Yet, so far, she had found no evidence of her cousin's involvement with Giacomo Ortoni. How marvellous if there were no connection whatsoever! It did seem possible.

Giacomo took a step towards her, that question still in his eyes, and she might have found it hard to deny her feelings for him if it had not been for Faustina.

There was a knock at Diana's bedroom door and a wrappered, be-curlered figure stood on the threshold. Every line of Faustina's tall, lean body was rigid with disapproval, and Diana, clutching her towel about her, knew her face was scarlet. Was there no privacy to be had here at all? Giacomo's family seemed overly possessive and intrusive.

'There have been raised voices this past half-hour,' Giacomo's great-aunt complained. 'Are you lost to all sense of discretion, Como? I would have thought, after that disgraceful affair with Ju . . .'

'Zia Faustina,' Giacomo interrupted, 'my apologies. I know appearances are against me. But you will appreciate that it is rarely Diana and I have a chance to be alone. I have just asked her to marry me.'

It was almost amusing, watching the gradual unbending of that austere figure. But Diana was far from feeling amusement. She was certain Faustina had been about to say 'Julia' and she was plunged into despair once more. The elderly woman moved further into the room to embrace first her great-nephew and then Diana.

'I am delighted,' she said warmly. 'I have always said you are too young, Como, to live alone. It only invites trouble from silly brainless fools of girls. And it would be a pity if our branch of the family were to die out. I do not like to think of Tancred's descendants living at Solamenza, which is what it would mean.' She turned to Diana. 'The inheritance is only through the male line. I hope you want children,' she said almost sternly. 'I know some of your countrywomen rebel against woman's prime function in life.'

Diana knew she was blushing again. She was also angry with Giacomo for putting her in this position. He had no right to let his aunt assume . . .

'Of course I want bairns some day,' she began, then, hastily because she was only adding credence to Giacomo's announcement, 'but the question doesn't arise, because I haven't said I . . .'

'Your arrival was a little inopportune, Zia Faustina.' Smoothly Giacomo intervened, cutting off Diana's denial. 'There was no opportunity for Diana to reply to my proposal.'

Faustina acknowledged his words with a slight bend of a head which, despite the curlers, still had a regal air.

'That may be so. However, I cannot think it suitable for you to be in Diana's room at this hour of the night. The Ortonis do not behave so. We have a reputation to uphold before our people. I suggest you postpone this matter until the morning.' And Faustina sat down on the edge of Diana's bed with every appearance of being prepared to remain there indefinitely.

Despite her inner turmoil, Diana could not help but be amused. It was quite something to see the autocratic Eagle of Solamenza being outfaced by the elderly woman. But though he was very much the head of his household it was evident that Giacomo respected his aunt, for he did withdraw, albeit with a bad grace, and Faustina rose to lock the communicating door behind him.

'And I suggest you lock the outer door too,' she told Diana, 'my nephew is a very determined man when he wants something.'

As Faustina showed signs of leaving Diana detained her. She felt bad about her position here, but she had to follow up every lead that offered.

'You said something when you came in—about a disgraceful affair?'

Faustina pursed her lips.

'Yes,' she admitted. 'But I spoke hastily—I was angry. And Como has forbidden us to speak of that incident. It is a matter to be forgotten,' she said firmly, 'for everyone's sake.'

'But it *was* to do with another woman?' Diana pressed, 'a . . . a girl?'

'There are some very foolish young women in the world,' Faustina said, and this time she made a more determined move towards the door. 'But that is all in the past now. It need not concern you and your relationship with Como.' As swiftly as she had entered, Faustina was gone. It was only too obvious that she was avoiding further questions.

Diana locked the door behind her as instructed, then sat down in a large, beautifully upholstered chair. Absently she traced the fabric design with her fingers. She was positive she had come close to finding out something about Julia. But how on earth was she to pursue the faint clue if all the Ortonis were sworn to silence? Moreover, she thought, with a plummeting heart, she didn't *want* to find out that Giacomo had been involved with Julia and her disappearance.

Despite the thickness of the castle's exterior walls, its elevated position meant chilly nights, and it was only when she realised how cold she was that Diana finally crept into bed. And even then she couldn't sleep. It was dawn before she slid into fitful slumber, to wake heavy-eyed and unrefreshed, reluctant to get out of bed.

She recognised the reluctance. It stemmed from the daunting knowledge of what she must face this morning.

Not only had she to face Giacomo himself, but also his family. She had no doubt that news of his proposal would have spread like wildfire through family and servants alike, with everyone assuming that of course she would accept.

Then, even if all the members of the family approved, there would be black looks from Assunta to be endured. And Maria? Maria who said nothing but overheard everything. The news would surely have reached her. And—unlike Faustina's reaction—the belief that Diana intended to marry her father would increase rather than decrease the child's resentment.

Her guess that the servants would be aware of overnight events was confirmed by the fascinated, wide-eyed stare of the small maidservant who unlocked the door and brought in the hot water for washing. Unlike yesterday's simple courtesy, this morning her obeisance held all the deference due to a future *contessa* of Solamenza. Whatever the rest of Italy might think about titles, here in *L'Aquila's* eyrie they still carried weight.

In rapid, voluble Italian, uttered in tones of extreme respect, the maid told Diana that the 'little *signorina*'s door had also been locked. This had given cause for concern as it was not usual. But she had opened it with a duplicate key. The little *signorina* was now washed and dressed and Luca had carried her downstairs. And when Signorina Watt was ready breakfast would be served.

This discreet hint told Diana that she was unpardonably late. She washed and dressed hastily and, trying to overcome her reluctance to face the Ortonis *en masse*, she descended the main staircase.

As she had feared, she had kept the whole family waiting. But there were no reproaches. In fact she was greeted with a warm affection that made her feel increasingly guilty. Only Maria studiously avoided her gaze, and Diana noticed that the child ate hardly any of the food set before her.

Diana found herself equally lacking in appetite. As befitted her supposed status as Giacomo's fiancée, she had been placed at his right hand, which did nothing to improve her state of nerves.

He, in contrast, was perfectly calm, eating heartily. He greeted Diana courteously as she sat down, but made no attempt at intimate conversation with her. Aware of the avid, sideways glances of his family, Diana was relieved.

Her relief was short-lived.

'Signorina Watt and I are going out. We will not be here for lunch,' he advised a glowering Assunta, who had punctuated her service at table with muttered, '*O miserias!*' 'But we will return in time for the evening meal.'

He was taking *her* agreement very much for granted, Diana thought indignantly, and she would have liked to protest. She didn't want to be alone with him all day. But she could hardly argue in front of the assembled family and the servants. She would bide her time.

But, breakfast over, he gave her no opportunity. He rose to his feet.

'Meet me outside in the courtyard in ten minutes,' he told Diana. 'Dress warmly—slacks, sweater, anorak. If there is anything you are short of Assunta will supply it.'

Diana had no wish to apply to the sullen housekeeper and she was glad her own wardrobe could provide these necessities. But the thought brought her up short. It presupposed that she intended to accompany Giacomo.

At first, as she made her way back to her room, she was tempted to stay there, to lock herself in if necessary. Giacomo could scarcely resort to physical force to make her go with him.

But that was the cowardly way out, and despite her present nervousness Diana had never been a coward. Best to face it out. She would go with him. But only because it would give her an opportunity of telling him she had no intention of marrying him—that in fact she was leaving his employ. She would demand that he send her back to Florence and from there she would go back to England.

With this fixed determination she changed out of her dress into warm woollen slacks and a sweater in a cheerful cherry-red. Her navy anorak over her arm, she was half-way downstairs again when she stopped.

She *couldn't* leave Solamenza yet. Last night she had almost certainly picked up the first—her only clue to Julia's fate. She continued the rest of the descent more slowly. She owed it to Aunt Marion to stay at Solamenza. But to do that she might have to accede to Giacomo's proposal. If she turned him down outright, the blow to his pride might make him dismiss her anyway.

'Most suitable! Red becomes you,' Giacomo told her. He was already in the courtyard, standing by its medieval moss-encrusted fountain, chatting to his remaining bodyguards. For a moment Diana thought Luca and Ubaldo might be going to accompany them, which would make any attempted intimacy or private conversation virtually impossible. But then, with a wave of his hand, Giacomo dismissed the two men.

'Are they not coming with us?' Diana must have sounded disappointed, for he looked at her quizzically.

'I thought you preferred not to be watched all the time?' Fortunately he didn't seem to expect an answer and went on, 'Protection is not necessary here. This is my own land, my own people. It would be a rash man who made any attempt upon me here,' he said as they made their way downhill through the narrow cobbled streets with their lime-washed houses to the town boundary, where the limousines were parked.

Diana could believe it. Affection and loyalty were very evident in the greetings he received. Women, clothed in black, seated on rush-bottomed chairs in doorways, sewing, knitting or lace-making, spoke to him with loving deference, as did the gossipy groups of menfolk.

To avoid the subject which must eventually be discussed and which she dreaded, Diana had resolved to quiz Giacomo again about his enemies. Before, when she had raised the subject, he had brushed it aside. But she was determined this time not to be put off.

'It's all to do with politics, isn't it,' she asked him, 'this need for protection?'

'You have learned this from my aunts, of course?' And as she nodded, 'They are all very proud of my uncle Sergio, and it is true there is great opposition in some quarters to Sergio's planned reforms.'

'What kind of reforms?'

'It is a question of public morality. I will not go into detail, but it is something about which Sergio and his followers have very strong feelings. If Sergio's legislation goes through it will make it harder for certain kinds of people to operate. Unfortunately,' Giacomo added wryly, 'one of his greatest opponents is a distant relative of ours—that other branch of the family I told you about.'

'Tancred's descendants?'

'*Si.*' They had reached one of the parked limousines and Giacomo opened the passenger door for her. As he took his place behind the wheel, he went on, 'If Sergio's ideas are made law, Vitto Ortoni will be one of the first to be put out of business. And though he too is a politician and as such should be above reproach, he has many dangerous contacts in the *bassifondi*—the underworld. Several attempts have been made on Sergio's life, but as a Minister he is too well protected. So Vitto and his cronies turned their attentions on me. Living in Florence, I was the only assailable member of Sergio's family.'

At the thought that Giacomo could easily have been assassinated, Diana felt her heart lurch sickeningly.

'And that's why you've made all the others stay at Solamenza?'

'*Si.* Sergio is a man of principle. He is not to be moved by threats to his own person. But if a member of his family were to fall into the hands of Vitto and his mercenaries . . .' Giacomo shrugged expressively.

'In that case, why did *you* stay in Florence for so long? Why didn't you and Maria come back here before?'

'I have certain affairs in Florence,' Giacomo said as he had told her before. 'They necessitate my presence there from time to time.'

Again his use of the word 'affairs' rather than 'business' made Diana think of other women, and inevitably that thought led again to Julia. She took the bull by the horns.

'What kind of affairs?' she asked bluntly, and was rewarded by one of his closed expressions.

'That is something I do not wish to discuss. Perhaps, if you were to become my wife . . .' He slanted her a sideways look. 'But then you do not wish to marry me, do you, Diana?'

'If you *know* that,' she said irritably, 'why on earth did you tell Zia Faustina . . . ? Why are you letting everyone else think . . . the rest of the family, the servants?'

'Because Zia Faustina was right. By being in your room last night I have compromised not only your reputation but mine. I told you, time has stood still in Solamenza. Old traditions still prevail. In such a situation as ours the only acceptable, honourable solution is marriage.'

'So now you want me to marry you just to save your face?'

He swore and braked hard, and the limousine veered over towards the edge of the narrow mountain road, making Diana gasp. But then she had other things to worry about, for Giacomo's hand was on her arm, its hard warm grasp punishing in its intensity. But it was not the pain she felt, only that fatal pull of the senses. She stared at him in mingled alarm and fascination.

'Diana!' There was both anger and reproach in his voice. 'I have also told you that I love you. That is the truth, the most important thing.' His hand released her arm, but only to slide up over her shoulder, to encircle the nape of her neck, making her shudder sensuously. 'It is also true, is it not, that you are physically attracted to me? No, do not deny it.' One finger of his free hand rested on her lips as they parted in protest. 'And I believe, given time, through the needs of your body, I could also teach you to love me. I have brought you out here—on our own—to ask you to at least agree to an engagement. That will be sufficient for the time being to silence the wagging tongues and to give us more time. I will try not to pressure you, Diana, *cara mia*.

What do you say?' He freed her mouth for speech.

Her voice was a nervous croak.

'I say, then suppose afterwards I find I can't love you? Or you might change *your* mind when you know more about me.'

'I doubt that,' he said gravely, 'but should it be so, then we will part with quiet dignity, admitting our mistake.' He bent his head and brushed her lips with his own. She could not quell her own leaping response and for a moment their mouths clung. Then, with a little sigh, he put her from him. 'It is very tempting to make love to you here and now, Diana, *cara mia*. But I have given my word not to rush you. So,' he suited the action to the word, 'we will drive on. We will spend this day together as friends, enjoying each other's company and our surroundings. And at the end of the day you will give me your answer, hmm?—whether we are to consider ourselves engaged?'

And he called that not rushing her! Diana thought half-humorously; she'd hate to see him when he was in a hurry.

She didn't answer his question. Instead she put one of her own.

'Where are we going?'

With a philosophical shrug Giacomo accepted her change of subject.

'I wish to show you more of our mountains—very different mountains, these.'

The destination he had in mind was the impressive dolomitic peaks, collectively known as the Gran Sasso, in winter the haunt of the skiing fraternity, in summer attractive to climbers. Long before they reached the foot of the mountain range Diana could see the aluminium-coloured towers of the cableway ascending the steep slopes of the southern wall of the mountain massif. Above them the cars swayed above precipices and vanished amid the still lingering snowfields.

The road they were following climbed to the lower station.

'We're . . . we're not going up there, are we?' she asked as Giacomo locked the car and with his hand tucked through her elbow led her towards the ground-level platform.

'But of course.' He urged her into one of the cable cars. 'Why do you think I told you to dress warmly?' He squeezed her arm. 'You are not afraid of heights?'

'No, but I've never been in one of these before.'

'Then you have a whole new experience ahead of you,' Giacomo told her. 'Together . . .' his voice dropped a suggestive octave, sending responsive shivers down her spine, 'we shall reach the heights, in this way if in no other.'

The steel and glass car was capable of holding about twenty people, but today they had it to themselves.

'The skiing is over until next winter,' Giacomo said as the ascent began.

At first it wasn't too bad. The scenery was certainly magnificent—the rugged skyline silvered by the blue air reflected on the snowcaps. But then the altitude became more alarming. As one car ascended a companion car descended, and where they met half-way the passage of each made the other rock slightly over an appalling gorge below. Diana gave a little cry of alarm and in an instinctive reaction buried her face against Giacomo's shoulder.

At once his arms went around her.

'You don't know, *cara mia*,' he murmured, 'how much it pleases me that you turn to me in this way. So you do not altogether mistrust me, hmm?' And as she lifted her head to apologise for her moment of foolishness he kissed her, not a fleeting caress this time but a long, sensual pressure that grew in intensity, making her forget the plunging depths below them, carrying her only to soaring heights.

If only this were all there was to it! she thought hazily. No mysteries, no suspicions, only this searing physical attraction, only love and a simple answer to be given. Yes. She didn't realise she'd said the word aloud against his mouth.

He raised his head and looked down into her eyes. His green ones were cloudy with desire.

'Yes?' he queried. 'To what are you saying yes?'

At once she withdrew from his embrace.

'I . . . I was just thinking aloud. Nothing important.'

'*Santa Maria*! You can think of unimportant things when I am kissing you!' He turned his shoulder on her, the picture of offended dignity, and gazed out over the surrounding peaks, but she had an idea he saw nothing.

She didn't blame him for being furious. It could be construed as an insult.

'I . . . I'm sorry,' she said contritely. 'That wasn't meant to be as rude as it sounded.' And in her haste to make amends she plunged over a precipice far deeper and more dangerous than those below her. 'It . . . it didn't mean I wasn't enjoying being kissed . . .'

'*Benissimo*!' He turned back, his eyes gleaming.

'But . . . but you did bring me up here to look at the scenery,' she added hastily.

Giacomo threw up his hands in mock despair.

'Never will I understand British women! There is passion there, yes, but you keep it battened down. You never allow it full rein. Even my Sandra,' he said with quiet sadness, 'had her private places to which I could not follow.'

If only *her* love for him were uncomplicated and admissible, Diana thought longingly, she would show him just how unfettered her passions could be. There would be no secrets she would withhold from him. To hide the betraying expression in her blue eyes she turned her attention to the mountains above and below them—and disguised a sigh in a gasp of admiration. Here were even more superb views. Rocks and corries known only to birds of prey; jagged pinnacles and lonely inaccessible valleys.

'The world of the eagle,' Giacomo said softly in her ear, 'where heaven and earth divide.'

Yes, she thought, and *he* was the eagle, for this was as much his world as was Solamenza, and she wanted oh, so desperately to share his world which he could make a heaven on earth for her.

The cable car slid into a little platform. It was bitterly cold up here and Diana was glad of her thick sweater and anorak. To her amazement Giacomo seemed to be proposing to walk further up the mountainside, and then, as they rounded a rockface, she saw a long, low building—a delightful wooden chalet with painted shutters.

'A hotel? Up here?' she exclaimed as he led the way to a flight of steps and into a blissfully warm foyer decorated with plants and beautiful modern paintings.

'*Si*. Skiers and climbers use it. I have stayed here once or twice myself.'

In the small lounge bar heated by a roaring fire, Giacomo ordered drinks and a meal. They were the only customers.

'Do you ski or climb?' asked Diana as she removed her anorak and perched herself on a high stool at the bar.

'Both.' He lifted his glass to her in a toast. 'To us!'

'You seem to lead a dangerous life one way and another,' she remarked.

'Believe me, *carissima*, the dangers I have experienced are as nothing when compared with loving you. I feel myself constantly on the brink of a crippling fall. If you refuse me . . .' His throaty voice broke off as if he could not contemplate the possibility, and Diana felt heat surge through her loins at the thought of his love and what marriage to him could mean. She lowered her eyes so that he could not see the blaze of emotion in their blue depths.

The bartender brought their meal, but though the food was good, Diana was scarcely aware of what she ate. She was conscious continually of Giacomo's eyes on her face, their caress sliding occasionally to her body, her breasts outlined by the taut woollen sweater so that she wished she had not removed her coat. She felt as naked before his scrutiny as she had the night before, clad only in a bathtowel. And he had seen her without the towel too, she remembered, and felt her face grow warm with the memory.

He was still watching her intently, and suddenly he put a hand on her knee. His clasp was warm even through the thick woollen cloth of her slacks, the pressure of his fingers meaningful. He looked around. The room was still empty, the bartender out of earshot. Even so he leaned closer.

'We could take a room here,' he said. 'We need not go back to Solamenza tonight. There would be no one to interrupt, to disapprove. I would have all the time in the world to show you . . . to teach you . . .'

'Como,' Diana said huskily, 'please . . . don't!'

'Why? Are you afraid? Of what? Of me? Of the attraction between us? You need have no fear. You must know I would never do anything to hurt you. Look at me, Diana, *amore mio*,' he pleaded, 'look at me, *per favore*. Tell me what I have to do, to say, to persuade you.'

She did meet his eyes, but despite very different inner feelings she schooled herself to keep her gaze cool and impersonal.

'There is nothing you can do or say,' she told him firmly, 'to make me sleep with you. I would have to be very, very sure to give myself to any man. And I'm not sure. Please accept that, Como.'

She wasn't certain if he'd taken in the full meaning of her words, for he pounced upon one particular phrase.

'"To give yourself to *any* man"? Does that mean you have never . . . ? That you are a virgin? That you have never made love to *anyone*?'

'Como! Please!' She was blushing furiously and her blonde head would have drooped once more, but his hand prevented it.

'Tell me!' he demanded.

'No, I . . . I've never . . .' she couldn't finish it because of the blazing triumph in his eyes.

'So,' he said softly, sensuously, 'I shall be the first with you. *Buono*. It is good.'

'You're taking an awful lot for granted.' She said it crossly because of the way he was making her feel.

'Perhaps, but I do not think so. I think that one day you *will* be mine. If you were totally uninterested in me you would not be here now . . .'

'I didn't have much choice,' she protested.

'. . . You would have given me a flat refusal,' Giacomo went on as if she hadn't interrupted. 'Oh, yes, Diana *carissima*, you would have made it very clear if I were distasteful to you. Your countrywomen are past mistresses of the art of the cold dismissal.'

To her relief he did not pursue the subject further. Instead he looked at his wristwatch.

'Well,' he shrugged philosophically, 'if you will not stay here with me tonight we must begin our journey home.' He stood up and lifted her down from the high bar stool, holding her for a moment before letting her slide the length of his hard body and making her aware just how much their conversation had aroused him. 'But we will come back to the Gran Sasso,' he promised, 'for our honeymoon. And I shall teach you to ski—among other things.'

'I thought the skiing was over,' she said pertly. It was time this intense conversation was lightened somehow. 'The new season is months away. So you must be prepared for a long wait.'

He caught up with her at the door and took her from behind in a bear-hug, his hands moving down over her stomach, over the bones of her hips, shaping and caressing them.

'I am *not* prepared for a long wait. It will be a long honeymoon,' he growled half playfully, half seriously.

The descent was not as alarming as the ascent had been. But even so Giacomo insisted on keeping his arm around Diana, making it difficult for her to concentrate on anything except his closeness. Behind them the mountains were sugar-pink in the setting sun.

'And what am I to tell my family?' he asked long before they reached ground level. 'Am I to tell them we are engaged?'

In spite of her bemused state, Diana *had* managed to give some thought to that question. As she had realised before, if she said no she must leave Solamenza. And though that might be the wisest course for her own peace of mind, it did not solve the problem of Julia.

Whereas, if she agreed, it gave her a cast-iron reason for staying. And if she stayed maybe she would discover that Julia's connection with the Ortinis was perfectly innocent. Giacomo or one of his aunts would be able to give her a forwarding address for her cousin.

And then—she caught her breath—the pretended engagement could become reality. She could actually *marry* Giacomo Ortoni!

Brushing aside the fearful alternatives, she looked at him.

'Aye, you can tell them we're engaged,' she said. Then, at the triumphant expression in his green eyes, the impulsive movement of his head towards her, 'if that's the only way to keep them happy. But as far as *we're* concerned it's only a trial. I'm still far from certain . . .'

'Forget your uncertainties,' Giacomo told her. 'I shall. For I *know* that you are going to marry me and that we are going to live as they do in the storybooks—happily ever after.'

CHAPTER SIX

EAGER, questioning faces greeted their return.

'She has accepted you, hasn't she?' Biella declared after one shrewd glance at her great-nephew. 'We must have a family celebration.' Excitedly, 'And Maria must be told!'

Only then did Diana realise the child wasn't present. Of course, it was past her bedtime. If she felt bad about the deception she was practising on Giacomo and on his family, she felt even worse about deceiving a child. Suppose Maria were to welcome her as a stepmother, Diana thought, and then circumstances forced her to leave Giacomo, to leave Italy . . .

'Please,' she begged, 'let me tell the bairn myself in my own way, tomorrow.'

'And do not stand any nonsense,' the more severe Faustina told her. 'If she is troublesome tell her she will be sent away to school again.'

Diana had no intention of making any such threat. She was hoping she could win the child round. Most of all she wanted to heal the breach between father and daughter. She was making plans, she realised with unhappy dismay, as though her future at Solamenza was assured, which it most certainly was not.

That night, even though Giacomo with great circumspection had wished her goodnight in front of his entire family, Diana still locked her door. Worried over the way events were sweeping her along, she was expecting to have a wakeful night, but her day out in the crisp mountain air had made her tired and she slept soundly and dreamlessly.

She rose early, determined to intercept Maria before anyone else could take the child downstairs. Her only greeting as she entered Maria's bedroom was a hostile stare from the green eyes so like Giacomo's and a firming of the petulant young lips.

Diana sat down on the edge of the bed.

'I know you're angry with me,' she addressed the silent figure, 'and I know you don't mean to speak to me. Very well. But you can hear me, and when I've told you everything I hope you'll understand. I want us to be friends again, Maria.'

She waited for a moment, giving the child a chance. But as there was no response she went on.

'What you saw—in my room the night before last—wasn't as bad as it looked. I don't want you to think I'm like the other girls you spoke of. I haven't been running after your father. But he . . . he says he's in love with me. He's asked me to marry him.'

Diana had expected resentment, anger even. What she was not prepared for was the expression of absolute horror that crossed the child's expressive little face.

'Maria,' she said pleadingly, 'I want you to know it's only a . . . a *trial* engagement. I . . . I'm not sure how I feel about Como. Things might not work out. And even if they do, I realise no one could ever replace your mother. I wouldn't even try. But I would like you and me to be friends.' She tried to bring a smile to the child's face. 'Wicked stepmothers only exist in fairy stories, you know!' This brought a response, but not the one Diana had hoped for.

'Yes, I know!' It came out as a strangled sob. 'But what

about wicked *fathers*?'

'Surely,' Diana said impulsively, 'you're not trying to tell me *your* father is wicked? I just don't believe it.' Then she bit her lip. Hadn't she come to Italy believing just that?

'You wouldn't believe it!' It was said with deep scorn. 'You *are* like the others. You think you're in love with him and . . .' tears began to trickle down the child's pale cheeks, 'you d-don't know as m-much about him as I do.' With a sudden despairing gesture the child buried her face in her pillow and gave way to such violent grief that Diana was alarmed.

'Maria,' she gathered the child up into her arms, 'you mustn't cry like that. You'll make yourself ill.'

'I'm n-not crying for myself,' the little girl choked against Diana's shoulder. 'I'm c-crying for you.'

'Goodness! You foolish bairn!' Diana tried to rally the child's spirits. 'Why should you cry over me? I'm perfectly all right.'

'I . . . I like you,' Maria sobbed. 'I don't want you to be made unhappy. I don't want anything to h-happen to you.'

'Nothing is going to happen to *me*.' Diana thought she understood. Maria had loved Sandra, her mother, but Sandra had died. The child was terrified of relating to anyone else, of loving again in case she lost again. Diana sighed. This didn't help her feelings of guilt. 'Maria . . .' she began, but a knock on the door heralded the arrival of the small maid with hot water. 'I'll help Maria wash and dress,' Diana told the young woman.

'Oh, no, *signorina*!' The maid's face registered disapproval. 'That would not be suitable. You are no longer an employee, but *L'Aquila's* intended. Besides, the Conte has asked me to give you a message. He wishes to see you before he leaves for Firenze.'

Diana caught her breath in alarm.

'He's going to Florence?' Giacomo had said nothing of this the previous day. Seized with a sense of urgency, Diana turned to the child. 'Maria, I have to see your father. We'll talk again after breakfast, eh?' She intercepted a strange look from the maid, who would not know of course that Maria had broken her silence.

'Como!' He was just crossing the main hallway, a briefcase in his hand, as Diana ran downstairs.

'Hmm?' He seemed preoccupied.

'I'm told you're going to Florence,' she said breathlessly. 'Is that wise? Oh, Como, do you *have* to go?' She couldn't keep the concern out of her face and eyes, and he jerked out of his introspection to smile wanly at her, putting an arm about her waist.

'It is good to know that you worry about me, *carissima*.' He dropped a kiss on the end of her nose. 'But have no fear, I shall come to no harm. Luca and Ubaldo go with me and I shall return tomorrow evening. Shall I bring you back an engagement ring from one of the jewellers on the Ponte Vecchio?'

'Oh, no!' she exclaimed. 'There's no need for that.' Then, hastily, 'I mean, there's no rush.' To actually wear his ring on her finger would only add to her sense of guilt.

'Perhaps you would rather wait until we can choose it together?' he suggested indulgently, and Diana leapt at the excuse.'

'Aye, that would be better. But that wasn't why you were going to Florence?'

'No. An important message came for me late last night.' He bent and brushed her lips in a warm but fleeting kiss. 'I must go.'

She followed him out into the courtyard.

'Is it this political matter again?'

'No, no. I beg you, Diana, do not concern yourself.'

'I wish I'd known earlier that you were going,' she said worriedly. 'I could have come with you.'

'I would not have taken you,' he told her sharply. And as she looked at him in wounded surprise he added a rider that to her acute ears was not altogether convincing, 'It is because you are too precious to me to risk your safety.' And with a salute of his hand he was gone.

'Take care!' she whispered, her fingers toying with the lucky black cat at her throat. She was gripped by the sense of fear that often obsessed lovers—that the safety of their loved one was only ensured when they were together.

'I suppose Como is off to Florence about his charity work as usual,' Biella said cheerfully over breakfast.

'Charity work?' queried Diana. This was something new.

'Has he not told you? That would be like him, of course. He has always been modest about his good works.'

'He believes—and I agree with him—that the possession of wealth entails responsibilities,' Faustina put in. 'You must know, Diana, that there is much poverty in southern Italy. Como has endowed a hospital and a nursing home for his less fortunate countrymen, as well as two orphanages in Florence.'

'And he will always help a sick foreigner in trouble,' added Biella. 'I wonder if he will visit the nursing home this time?' And to Diana, 'There are some tragic cases there. We know of . . .'

'He visits each of them regularly,' Faustina put in—rather hastily, Diana thought, and the older woman cast a rather strange look at Stefano, 'to see that they are being run as they should be. He pays particular attention to the orphanages. He is very fond of children.'

A stifled sound from Maria drew everyone's attention, but the child's face was an inscrutable blank.

'That child is not eating properly again,' Faustina said irritably. 'She has hardly touched her breakfast. Really, I do not know what is to be done with her!'

'She'll eat when she's hungry,' Diana said gently with a comforting smile at Maria. Then to the child, she said, 'Maria, I still haven't seen the whole of the castle. I'd particularly like to see the private gardens. As it's such a nice day perhaps you'd show me around?'

'And how is she to do that, pray?' Faustina enquired caustically.

'I think I can manage the wheelchair on my own,' said Diana.

'The grounds are on different levels.'

But Diana was determined not to be put off.

'Maria isn't very heavy. I'm sure I could carry her up a few steps.'

As they left Stefano and the great-aunts and uncles lingering over a second cup of coffee, Maria pulled at Diana's sleeve.

'There's something else I'd like to show you before we go outside,' she murmured. 'This way.' She pointed to a corridor at right angles to the one they were traversing.

At the far end of the corridor Maria indicated a heavy oak door. It opened into a room furnished as a study and library—Giacomo's territory, obviously. But he had never brought Diana here, and she felt a little uneasy at this trespass.

'What did you want to show me?' she asked.

Maria pointed to a large oil painting that hung between two narrow wings facing the desk. The work portrayed a tall, slender woman, darkly beautiful with shoulder-length auburn hair and large widely spaced grey eyes that stared back at the onlooker with grave serenity. Her generously formed mouth was curved into a slight smile.

As she studied the portrait Diana knew a sense of foreboding. She could guess the name of the subject—Sandra, Maria's mother. But what struck her forcibly was the striking resemblance to someone she knew as well as she knew her own mirror-image. With a change of hair colour and more intensity of expression it could have been her cousin Julia.

In an attempt to shake off her uneasiness, she turned to Maria with a smile.

'I can see where you get your lovely hair. It *is* your mother, isn't it?'

The child was gazing broodingly up at the painting.

'Yes. Do you think she was beautiful?'

'Very. And you will be too some day.'

But the little girl didn't seem to be seeking reassurance on that point.

'Then why did he stop loving her?' she wanted to know.

'I'm sure he didn't,' said Diana. 'Just because he's planning to get married again it doesn't mean . . .'

'Oh, I know that! I don't mean because of you. He stopped loving her a long time ago—he must have done!'

Diana sighed and leant against the edge of the leather-tooled desk.

'Maria,' she said firmly, 'I think it's time you stopped dropping all these obscure hints. I'm not a mind-reader. Just tell me, simply and clearly, please—what is it you have against your father and why you think he stopped loving your mother?'

There was misery in the young face and the green eyes turned towards Diana. But Maria's answer could not have been more direct and more horrifying.

'Because he killed her.'

For a moment Diana could not speak or move. And when she did move the child flinched away from her as if she expected a blow. Instead Diana placed her hands on Maria's shoulders and looked earnestly into the pale heart-shaped face on which every freckle stood out individually.

'Look at me, Maria!'

The child's eyes, now that she knew she was not to be punished, met Diana's fearlessly.

'You really believe that, don't you?' Diana said wonderingly. 'You're *not* just saying it to get rid of me.'

'I don't want to get rid of you,' Maria told her. 'I'd like you to stay if only you weren't going to marry *him*.' She nodded towards a companion portrait that Diana had not noticed, and she released the child's shoulders and moved to look at it.

Was that the face of a murderer?

From the portrait Giacomo Ortoni stared back at her, the green eyes as inscrutable as in life, the sensual mouth slightly smiling. It was a handsome face, an intelligent face. Diana weighed Maria's image of him against what *she* knew of him—autocracy leavened by sensitivity of nature, his responsible attitude towards his elderly dependants, his charitable work. His unrequited affection for his small daughter. It just didn't add up.

She turned back to the child.

'How do you *know* your father killed your mother?'

'I heard him say so,' Maria said simply. And then, 'I expect he killed Julia too.'

'*What?*' Diana's stomach lurched, her head spun and for a moment she thought she was going to faint. She sat down abruptly in a large leather chair. 'What did you say?'

'I said he probably killed Julia too. She disappeared very suddenly.'

'Who . . . who was Julia?' asked Diana, though she knew very well.

'One of the girls who came to look after me. She wasn't bad—she made me laugh. She reminded me of my mother a bit. She was the only one, besides you, that I talked to.'

Diana had to ask.

'And . . . and was *she* interested in your father?'

'Oh, yes,' Maria said with great certainty. 'They all were.'

Diana felt a desperate need to get out of this room, to get out of the immuring walls of the castle which was beginning to feel like Bluebeard's lair. Any moment now and Maria would be telling her that all of her companions had mysteriously disappeared. Fresh air was a great restorer of sanity, she had always found.

With one last look at the portraits, she turned the wheelchair and they left the study. Her legs still felt decidedly wobbly as they returned the way they had come, and in the main hall they met Stefano.

'W-would you like me to help with the wheelchair?' he asked.

'There's no need,' Diana assured him. But her voice must have sounded rather shaky, because he said with rather pathetic earnestness, 'I d-don't have anything more important to d-do. I'd really l-like to help.'

Diana always felt obscurely sorry for Stefano. Set alongside the strong personalities of his brother and the aunts and uncles, he seemed a shadowy, insubstantial figure. His manner was one of self-effacement, particularly when Giacomo was around. She had no objection to Stefano accompanying them on their tour of the castle grounds. But what about Maria? The presence of her uncle would undoubtedly silence her. But perhaps that might be a good thing. Diana didn't feel she could cope with any more revelations for the moment. She turned to the child with raised eyebrows.

'Shall we let Uncle Stefano help?'

Maria didn't speak, but she gave a not ungracious nod. Obviously she had no particular animus against her father's younger brother.

Their way led through the courtyard with its ancient fountain, around two sides of the hexagonal building and through a small gateway set in a wall. It was an unpromising enough entrance into an enchanted place.

'Goodness!' exclaimed Diana. 'I never expected it to be anything like this!'

The garden, though small, had been designed to give a feeling of spaciousness. Built on several levels, each terrace was hedged with box and ornamented with low balustrades and urns. At strategic points marble seats invited the spectator to take his or her ease before this or that pleasing prospect—a sculptured divinity, a fountain surrounded by posturing Tritons and naiads.

'It was n-not always this way,' Stefano told her. 'Como had a man come out here f-from Florence. Sandra and the designer p-planned it together, to remind her—on a miniature scale—of her family's h-home in England.'

'She must have come from a wealthy family?' Diana guessed.

'She was a c-considerable heiress,' Stefano agreed. 'Her p-parents' death left her with a vast fortune.'

A horrible serpent of suspicion crawled around Diana's already queasy stomach. Murders had been committed for much less than a fortune. And yet Giacomo was rich in his own right, wasn't he?

With Stefano carrying the wheelchair and Diana carrying Maria, they mounted slowly from terrace to terrace until they reached the penultimate level. Here there was a sudden change of mood that was more in keeping with the way Diana felt than the rest of the sunlit garden.

Above them, at the top of crumbling stone steps, untrimmed hedges loomed gloomily high, flanking a tall iron gate fastened by a heavy padlock and chain.

'What's behind there?' asked Diana.

Stefano shot a swift, almost furtive glance at Maria. But the child was engrossed in watching a green lizard, frozen into immobility in a crevice of the sun-baked stones.

'*Il cimitero.*'

'A cemetery!' Diana exclaimed. 'At the end of your garden?'

'It is the f-family resting place,' Stefano explained. 'It has b-been there since the time of Rainulf Ortoni. His enemies would have thought nothing of d-desecrating Ortoni graves. So they were sited within the castle walls.'

'There are graves in there going back to the eleventh century? How fascinating!' Diana tried to peer through the iron gate, but the turn of a path winding between guardian cypresses obscured her view. 'I'd love to see them. Can we go in?'

'It is locked,' Stefano reminded her.

'Can't we get the key?'

'Except for the g-gardener no one goes in unless there is a funeral.'

'So it's still in use today?' Diana lowered her voice. 'Is . . . is Sandra buried there?'

'Of c-course.'

And who else? she wondered with a superstitious

shudder.

'And it's only for family graves?'

'And s-servants or employees. And n-now could we talk about something less m-morbid?' Stefano shivered and his stutter had become more pronounced. 'I hate talk of d-death or illness.' His olive complexion had paled, and Diana understood why Faustina had changed the subject of the breakfast-time conversation so abruptly.

Somewhat reluctantly she turned away from the cemetery gates. Stefano was trying to draw her attention to the prospect of the flint and granite town below them and the enormous curves of the mountains beyond.

Far, far below, the road, reduced to a pygmy highway, wound over the rugged terrain.

'In the days of those old family feuds they must have been able to see their enemies coming for miles,' Diana commented.

'What makes you think the f-feud is over?' Stefano asked somewhat bitterly. 'It is ridiculous in this d-day and age. I would like to see an end of it.'

'Have *you* met the other branch of the family?'

'*Si*. In Rome—at a party—I met our cousins Iolanda and Vitto.' To Diana's amazement Stefano flushed scarlet and again his stammer was more in evidence. 'I c-cannot approve of V-Vitto, of course, b-but I thought his sister Iolanda rather splendid. W-we got on very well. I still cannot believe . . .' But he broke off at this interesting point.

Shrewdly, Diana guessed that Stefano was more than a little in love with his cousin. But having met Iolanda—and family feud apart—she thought it an unlikely match. Iolanda the forceful businesswoman would eat the timid Stefano alive!

They sat for a while on one of the marble seats that commanded the best view over the Abruzzi countryside. But as the sun grew hotter Diana with her fair complexion had to admit defeat, and at her request they sought the protection of the castle walls.

The rest of the day seemed long, and Diana had to admit to herself that it was Giacomo's absence that made the time drag tediously. The Ortoni family, Maria included, observed the siesta period that afternoon. But Diana, as always, found it difficult to sleep by day. Left to her own resources, she had plenty of time to think, and the subject uppermost in her mind was Maria's accusation against her father.

If this had been England and Giacomo any ordinary man of her acquaintance she would have pooh-poohed the whole idea. But though she knew him better now, Giacomo was still a bit of a mystery man. And he himself had described this place as one where time had stood still, where strange observances took place. And given the intense feudal loyalty of his family and his followers, she supposed even the concealment of a murder was possible. Two murders? And yet her intuition—or was it her infatuation? she asked herself sceptically—told her that Giacomo Ortoni was no murderer.

That evening she would have liked to quiz Biella, as the most talkative and indiscreet member of the Ortoni family, about the family cemetery. But she could never seem to get Giacomo's great-aunt to herself. But as she prepared for bed that night she was determined that somehow she was going to see inside that padlocked gate.

'The cemetery?' asked Biella in tones of amazement when Diana cornered her next morning after breakfast. 'Why on earth do you want to go in there?' She shuddered dramatically. 'Life is too short to be thinking about such things! But then,' she relented, 'you are still young. I suppose it does not trouble you as much as it does us older folk.'

'It's not just morbid curiosity.' Reluctantly Diana uttered the untruth. 'It must be very interesting, historically.'

'I suppose so,' Biella conceded. 'Well, my dear, if you want to go in you will have to approach Pasquale, Assunta's husband. He is the gardener and he also tends the graveyard.'

Diana quailed at the thought that she might have to make the approach to Assunta's husband through the hostile housekeeper. There had been no more superstitious gestures made in her direction; perhaps Giacomo had issued instructions. But there was no doubt the elderly woman still resented her. However, by assiduously haunting the garden from time to time she finally found Pasquale working there. Siesta was over and he was making use of the cooler evening to catch up on his work.

Pasquale was a quiet, slow-thinking and speaking man, an unlikely husband for the fierce and voluble Assunta. He seemed stolidly unsurprised when she asked for the key to the iron gate. He was probably resigned to female domination, Diana felt.

There was no time to make use of the key before the evening meal. But immediately afterwards, Diana resolved, she was going to satisfy the curiosity she had denied.

'I thought Giacomo said he would be home this evening,' Faustina said to no one in particular over the post-dinner coffee. 'I hope all is well with him.'

'Perhaps his visits took longer than he expected,' Biella said cheerfully. 'He is probably staying an extra night. Much safer to drive over these roads in the daylight.'

Diana was torn. With one part of her she longed for Giacomo to return. She missed him, and she knew she craved the sensation of being in his arms again, of being kissed by him. Somehow, in his presence, all her doubts of him were reduced to nonsense. It was only when she couldn't see him that the dark fears took over, making her lend credence to all kinds of suspicions. But set against her need to see him was the knowledge that if he returned it would be impossible for her to visit the cemetery.

As soon as she decently could she slipped away from the family gathering with an excuse about checking up on Maria.

It was not quite dusk as she made her way across the courtyard and slipped through the garden door. With no child to carry this time she made swift work of the climb to the upper terrace. Then, carefully, she mounted the final broken stone staircase. Weeds grew in the gaps the steps had made as they crumbled. With trembling fingers she inserted the heavy battered antique key into the padlock. It turned easily.

The path through the overhanging cypresses was narrow, their fronds brushing her cheek like ghostly fingers. Mercifully it was short, opening out upon the prospect of a small chapel—something she had not expected. But of course, in times of siege, the family would have needed somewhere to worship. Presumably, nowadays, they used the more modern building down in the town.

She had expected the chapel, like the cemetery, to be locked, but its stout door yielded easily to her hand. Predictably it was dark inside and she wished she had thought to bring a torch. However, the last visitant had thoughtfully left a box of matches beside a row of candles.

The candlelight was just sufficient to show her the still

brilliant and sumptuous frescoes that covered the chapel walls. They were more pagan than religious—nymphs and fauns, animals and flowers—and again Diana was reminded that these were a superstitious people and her fingers felt for the reassurance of her lucky charm. And as she did so something seemed to lunge at her out of the shadows above.

Startled, she gave a little scream and stumbled, grasping at a carved pew to save herself. A bat, disturbed by the light and her presence, swooped back and forth below the vaulted roof. In daylight it might not have troubled her; she knew and discounted all the old myths about bats becoming entangled in women's hair. But at night its silent flight seemed menacing, adding to the skin-prickling atmosphere of the place.

Diana didn't believe in such things. But she had once, out of curiosity, attended a séance and she was sensitive by nature. This place struck her as being haunted by Ortonis down the ages.

'And by goodness knows who else,' she muttered to herself.

Hurriedly she left the chapel. The light was fading and she knew she must not loiter if she were to have time to study the drunken rows of lichen-encrusted headstones. Some of them, as she had expected, were incredibly old and she would have liked to spend more time over them. But, contrary to what she had told Biella, she was not here for ancient history.

She made her way deeper into the cemetery through rows of high pedestals supporting busts and towering angels that seemed about to lunge at the passer-by. The headstones were growing more modern in appearance, their inscriptions more legible, and at last she found what she was looking for—a simple white piece of marble. The black lettering leapt out at her: 'Sandra—*in pacem in aeternam*'. Below were given the dates of birth and death. Sandra had been only twenty-five when she had died.

Diana translated the words beneath the dates into her own language. 'Beloved wife of Giacomo Ortoni—deeply mourned and never forgotten'.

There were more words below, partly obscured by a flowering shrub that had been planted on the grassy mound. Diana bent lower and held the fronds aside.

'. . . and their son, Giacomo, one hour old. God gave and took away.'

The words were simple without the floweriness one sometimes saw on such stones, but Diana was deeply moved. Tears pricked behind her eyes and she sank to her knees in front of the grave.

'Poor baby,' she murmured, 'poor Sandra . . . and poor Giacomo—to lose his son as well.' From what Faustina had said she could guess how important a son and heir would have been to him.

But it was growing darker and she still had one more thing to do. She rose to her feet and checked the rest of the graves. More aunts and uncles, ancient retainers with the inscription 'good and faithful servant'. But that was all. Well, what did you expect, she asked herself ironically—'Julia—*in pacem in aeternam*' as well? That would have been too easy. Julia was neither family nor retainer. An *au pair* girl would scarcely qualify for burial here.

Diana was glad when she had negotiated the cypress-lined path and passed through the outer gate. Carefully she closed it behind her and fumbled with the lock. It was not as easy to secure as it had been to open. She had just breathed a sigh of relief at the reassuring click that told her

the hasp had finally gone home when she felt herself
grasped from behind.

A heavy hand rested on each shoulder. Diana screamed
and found herself jerked around to face her assailant.

'*Madre di Dio*! What do you think you are doing there?'

'*Como*! Oh!' Relief weakened knees already tremulous
with the fright he'd given her and she sagged against him.
But he put her away almost roughly.

'What were you doing in there? Who gave you leave?'

'N-no one really,' she stammered. 'I just borrowed the
key.'

'From whom?' he demanded angrily. 'From Pasquale?
Dio, has the man no sense?'

'Oh, please, you mustn't blame him. He probably
thought I had your permission.'

'Impossible! He knows better than that.'

'I didn't mean any harm,' Diana told him. 'I . . .'

'Maybe not. But you might have *come* to harm. The place
is a deathtrap—crumbling steps, monuments leaning and
ready to fall at any moment.'

Diana looked up at him doubtfully. 'Is that the only
reason you're angry?'

'Of course.' His taut features had relaxed a little and his
eyes were quizzical. 'What other reason should I have?'

She could hardly tell him that she had attributed his
anger to a guilty secret.

'Oh . . . I don't know. I thought maybe you thought me
impertinent, thought I was prying.'

'Diana, *cara mia*,' his hands on her shoulders had gentled
now, 'what I own is yours. I marvel at your wish to visit my
decayed ancestors, but if that is your desire, so be it. All I
ask is that you pay your respects in daylight and
accompanied. Suppose you had met with an accident? You

could have been there till morning. And you know how cold it is on these mountains at night.'

'How did you know where to find me?' she asked as, his arm about her waist, they negotiated the steps of the many terraces.

'Fortunately,' Giacomo said drily, 'Pasquale tells Assunta everything.'

'I bet he wouldn't dare not to,' Diana said involuntarily.

Giacomo laughed, that warm sound that she loved. How could she ever have believed any ill of this man? she thought, nestling against him.

'Probably not,' he agreed. 'I hope you have no ideas of being a dominating wife, *carissima*? For I warn you I am made of sterner stuff than Pasquale.'

Diana pulled a little away.

'Our . . . our marriage isn't *definite*,' she reminded him anxiously.

'Not to you, perhaps,' he said with easy assurance, 'but I am confident you will come round to my way of thinking. Especially,' he stopped in a shadowy corner of the garden and drew her into his arms, 'especially when I have made love to you a few more times.'

An ache began deep in the pit of her stomach as he kissed her and went on kissing her until she was trembling in his arms, pressed hard against the masculinity of his body.

Her arousal seemed to make all her senses more aware. It was dark now and moonlight spilled itself over archways and ancient doorways. Scents from the garden herbs assailed her nostrils. Somewhere in the town below a tenor voice was singing—'O sole mio' and from the campanile of the church a bell rang. It was a moment of beautiful poignancy.

Giacomo must have been aware of it too, and he

confirmed her thought as his kisses, his caresses became more urgent.

'Do not keep me waiting too long, *bella mia*,' he pleaded huskily. 'Do not let your doubts and fears stand between us and happiness.'

Doubts and fears. That summed it up so exactly. And Giacomo was right, procrastination was not the way to allay them.

'Como?' she said tentatively.

'*Si, carissima*?' He leaned a little away and looked down into her face. 'You sound suddenly very earnest.'

'I want to ask you something,' she told him, staring fixedly at his chest. 'But I'm afraid you'll be offended, or hurt.'

He slid a gentle finger down the soft curve of her cheek and hooked it beneath her chin, lifting it so that she had to return his gaze.

'I am sure, Diana, that you would never willingly offend or hurt anyone. You have too gentle, too caring a nature. But it must be something very important to you that you are willing to take that risk?'

'It is important. It's about . . . about Sandra.' She waited fearfully for his body to stiffen with annoyance—or some other emotion, but he remained quite relaxed, his expression in the moonlight mildly enquiring. 'I . . . I saw her grave in the cemetery. Como,' she took a deep steadying breath, 'how did she die?'

Now that the question was out her heart was fluttering frantically like a panicky bird. Now, surely, he would be angry.

He pulled her back into his arms and she felt his chest lift in an enormous sigh. He rested his cheek against the top of her head.

'I have wondered whether you would ask me that. Diana, I do not want you to be frightened. You have my promise, if you marry me, that you shall not die in the same way.'

Oh, God! What had she started? What was he about to tell her? Diana trembled. Giacomo held her from him again and looked down at her.

'You *are* afraid of that?' he said. 'Diana, I have sworn that I will never subject any woman to that ordeal again. Family traditions are as nothing . . .'

'Traditions? Ordeal?' Diana knew her voice was squeaky. All her superstitious nature to the fore, she wondered what dreadful practices he was about to reveal.

'I wanted a son, Diana . . . a male heir to inherit all of this,' he gestured to their surroundings. 'Sandra had a bad time when Maria was born. The doctors warned us it could be dangerous for her to have another child. And yet,' his voice was filled with self-loathing, 'I got her pregnant again. Sandra died in childbirth, Diana. *I* killed her.'

'Oh!' Diana exclaimed, and again she sagged with relief and for a moment could say nothing else.

'You have my word for it,' Giacomo said anxiously, 'there will be no more children.'

'Och, Como!' She was able to speak now and she looked up at him tenderly. 'I'm not afraid of that . . .'

'But I am,' he said. 'And I've never ceased to blame myself for . . .'

'Como,' she interrupted him excitedly, 'have you ever said that to anyone before?'

'What? That I will never subject another woman . . .?'

'No, no . . . that you felt responsible . . . that you killed Sandra. Have you ever actually put it to anyone in those exact words?'

'More than once, I expect,' he said gloomily. 'In those

first few days after she died I was beside myself with grief and remorse.'

'Could . . . could Maria have overheard you?'

'I don't know. I . . .' He stopped short. And then, as though her excitement had communicated itself to him, 'Why?' he demanded urgently. 'Why do you ask?'

'Oh, Como!' Diana clutched at the front of his shirt. 'I think . . . Oh, I hope I'm right. I think I know why Maria behaves towards you as she does.'

Giacomo was certainly quick on the uptake.

'You mean she must have heard . . . ? She must have thought . . . ?'

'Yes. She's only a bairn, and bairns have vivid imaginations. They misunderstand. Oh, Como, let's go and see her now, tell her . . .'

'She will be asleep,' he protested.

'Och, what does that matter?' Diana was impatient. 'This is important. Perhaps the most important thing in her life—your life.'

'Important, yes,' he agreed, 'but you, Diana, you are the *most* important. I think I knew, the first time we met— that day in Florence—that you would bring me good luck.'

'Even though you're not superstitious,' she teased. Then, 'Please, Como, let's go and see Maria and find out if I'm right.'

'And if you are wrong?'

But Diana was filled with confidence.

'I'm right. I just know I am.'

An hour later, Diana went to bed with the happy knowledge that she had brought father and daughter together.

Suspicious at first, Maria had nevertheless listened, as

Diana explained for her in simple terms how her mother had died and how Giacomo had blamed himself, his unfortunate choice of words. And when Maria, with happy tears, had cast herself into Giacomo's arms, Diana crept unnoticed from the bedroom, her own eyes threatening to overflow.

She was in bed, but she could not sleep. At last she heard the door of Maria's room close and Giacomo's footsteps as he went along the passageway. They did not pause outside her door as she had half thought they might, and she stifled a sigh. It was better so.

Then she heard a gentle tapping on the communicating door, which had remained firmly locked ever since that first night when Faustina had made her dramatic entrance.

'Diana!'

She slid out of bed and ran to the door, pressing her face against its unyielding panels. Beneath the thin stuff of her nightdress her breasts rose and fell agitatedly.

'Como?' she said breathlessly.

'Thank you, Diana. From the bottom of my heart, thank you.'

'That's all right.' Just the sound of his voice, the knowledge that only a few inches of wood divided them, made her tremble.

There was a long silence, then, 'Diana?'

'I'm still here.'

'This is no way to tell you of my gratitude. I want to thank you properly.' Silence again, and Diana quivered, knowing what he would say next. 'Diana, will you unlock the door? Just for a few moments. I do not ask any more, I give you my promise.'

But, entirely forgetting her scanty attire, she was already busy with the key, and he had not finished speaking when she opened the door to him.

It was so natural to go straight into his arms.

'*Amore mio*,' he whispered as he held her tightly. 'If it had not been for your sensitive, perceptive nature, your courage in speaking of it, I might never have discovered what separated me from Maria.'

'I'm so glad I was able to help.'

'Such courage can only be born of a loving nature,' he told her. 'Diana, was it for love of Maria that you spoke to me? Or can I dare to hope . . . ?'

It was not often, she knew, that Giacomo was at a loss for words. That he was now was proof of the intensity of his feelings. How Diana wished she could tell him what he wanted to hear, and if she could have listened only to her heart's promptings she *would* have told him the truth—that she wanted him as much as he wanted her—that she loved him. But there was still an unanswered question, and this one she simply dared not ask him. What had happened to Julia?

But her fear stemmed from a different motive now. Now that Sandra's death had been logically explained she no longer believed that any sinister fate had befallen her cousin. But if she questioned Giacomo the truth must also come out about herself and the reason for her presence in Italy. And he would be quite within his rights to cast her out in scorn and anger.

No. Somehow she must find out about Julia just as she had planned to all along—on her own initiative.

CHAPTER SEVEN

'DIANA?' Then, more forcefully, '*Diana*! You have gone away from me!' Giacomo, she realised, was still waiting for his answer.

'I'm sorry,' she said penitently. 'But I *was* thinking about your question.'

'And?' There was hardly suppressed impatience in his voice, and the silk robe he wore did nothing to disguise the urgency in the virile lines of his body.

'Como,' she begged, 'I have to ask you to be patient with me a little longer. I just *can't* rush into something as important as marriage. I feel I was wrong in agreeing to an engagement—even a trial one.'

'You are not trying to back out of it?' His tone had become ominous.

'N-no,' she said doubtfully, and then as his grip tightened and he growled an imprecation in his throat, 'of . . . of course not. If I make a bargain I keep it. I will give it a fair trial. But that means you must keep your promise too—not to rush me.'

He put her from him and folded his arms as though that was the only way he could restrain himself. But his expression was grim.

'I have to say I cannot see your difficulty,' he said. 'I have no doubt that *I* love *you*. Either *you* love *me* or you do not. It is black or white, surely? There can be no shades of grey.'

Diana sought desperately for an answer that would satisfy

him. And in all fairness, she decided, only the truth would suffice.

'Como, I *do* love you. No,' as his face lit up and he would have moved towards her again, 'please hear me out. I . . . I'm physically attracted to you, I admit that. And I know that's part of love. But there's more to it than that. Sometimes love on its own isn't enough to base a whole lifetime on. There has to be liking too, and trust . . .'

'Are you saying you do not like me?' There was displeasure in every line of his taut body. 'What have I done to deserve that?'

'Nothing! At least, I hope not. And I *do* like you. Oh, please don't misunderstand me. I just feel we ought to be sure we can be friends as well as lovers.' She sought desperately for further reasons to convince him. 'There might be things about *me* that *you* don't like. Don't you see, I'm trying to be fair to you as well as to myself?'

'And how much longer,' sarcastically, 'is this "getting to know each other" process to continue?'

'I don't know,' she confessed.

He was growing increasingly irritable.

'I am beginning to suspect you of trifling with me, Diana. Is there some selfish motivation of yours about which I do not know? Is this what I may not "like" about you?'

Oh, but he was perceptive!

'I can be selfish too,' he warned her. 'And by nature, I am not a patient man, especially when I want something. And just so that you are in no doubt about my impatience . . .'

His kiss was like the initial spark that lights a devastating conflagration, shocking her not only by its violence but by her equally violent response to it.

He pressed her against him, forcing her awareness of his stirring masculine desire that surged hard and strong against her stomach. The fierce heat of desire, never far from the surface when he was near, blazed up in her. Her arms crept around his strong neck, her body bent to his, and beneath her flimsy nightdress her breasts became hard, painful buds.

Her reaction inflamed him further and his hands spread hungrily over her buttocks, kneading the soft flesh, and then, before she could guess at his intention, he had lifted her in his arms, his heart thudding unevenly against her cheek, and carried her through to his bedroom. There he tumbled her into the centre of the bed—a vast *letto matrimoniale*—pinning her there with his own weight.

'No, Como, please . . .' she struggled to rise. 'You promised . . .'

'And you made a promise to me, *carissima*—the fulfilment of which seems to recede further and further away.'

'It was only forty-eight hours ago,' she protested. 'Some people are engaged for up to a year or . . .'

'You want our engagement to last for a year?' He did not give her a chance to answer yes or no but began to kiss her again, draining all her will to resist, pressing her softness against the excitingly hard lines of his body. He was warm and clean-smelling, and his closeness was making her delirious with love, with mingled pleasure and pain.

'*How* long do you want to wait?' he asked again, but once more she was not allowed the right of reply, his mouth smothering hers.

His hands moved over her body, brushing aside the thin straps of her nightdress, laying bare her soft flesh to his marauding mouth. She shivered as his lips became absorbed with her breasts, lightly and exploratively. She could feel the desire beating higher and higher within his body.

'Still want to wait, Diana?' His hand brushed the calf of her leg, then moved upwards beneath her nightdress, reaching the tender curves of her soft thigh, the swell of her stomach. Her skin was acutely sensitive to his touch, and when his hand reached her hip she gasped at the almost painful response she felt.

As his hand moved on she shuddered convulsively and her breathing grew more rapid, keeping pace with his. She felt the beads of moisture spring out on her forehead and upper lip. Her heart was thudding noisily, suffocating her.

Her shivering intensified as Giacomo's hand sought further intimacies, sending pleasure shooting along every sensitised nerve. She knew where this was leading them, but with her will-power distorted by his proximity she could do nothing to prevent it. All her inhibitions seemed drowned in this irresistible delight and she found herself returning his caresses, as eager to learn about his body as he was to discover hers.

Beneath his robe his olive skin, damp with perspiration, was smooth over hard bone and muscle. It pleased her exploring fingertips. Roughened chest, flat, firm stomach. Down . . . down . . . and ah . . . ! Oh, he was magnificent! His sudden indrawn breath and slight shudder invoked an instant response in her. Her body seemed to have taken on a will of its own, straining and stretching to meet his as though this might ease its awful agony.

'*Shall* we wait a year, *cara mia*?' Between his harsh jagged indrawn breaths he murmured the question against her lips. His voice was barely audible and long, violent tremors shuddered through him.

'No! Oh, no!' Dizzy with desire, Diana clung to him as he threatened to draw away from her. But he was only discarding his robe. He was going to make her his—now.

She knew it, and she had no wish to stop him. Problems that had loomed large seemed insignificant beside the wanting that drove their bodies.

'Then tell me you love me,' he commanded. 'Tell me you want me. Tell me you don't want to wait.'

'I love you—oh, Como, I love you,' she murmured brokenly.

'You *want* me,' he insisted, and when she complied, 'and you don't want to wait.'

'I don't want to wait,' she gasped, and then the full weight of his aroused body was on hers. She arched urgently beneath him, welcoming the heated pressure, her soft moans encouraging him.

The ache within her built up to explosion point until, just as she thought she could bear no more, Giacomo possessed her in a long, sweet, agonising culmination of feeling.

For a moment afterwards his weight remained upon her, limp with exhaustion, then he rolled away with a muttered imprecation.

'*Dio*, but I am a fool!' he berated himself. 'Forgive me, Diana!'

'What for? What's wrong?' She was totally drained herself, barely able to turn her head on the pillow to look at his taut features.

'In my desire for you, *carissima*, I forgot . . . I took no precautions.' His dark eyes were haunted. 'If I have made you pregnant . . .'

Lovingly Diana put her hand against his cheek.

'It doesn't matter, Como, truly,' she murmured. A heavy languor had followed her initiation into physical love and she was on the verge of sleep. 'I'm very healthy and I'm not afraid. I *want* to have your bairns.'

'*Amare mia*,' she heard him whisper brokenly as she

drifted into slumber.

The early morning sunlight woke her. Shafting through the leaded window, it dappled their naked bodies and the bed—Como's bed. And the events of last night came flooding back to Diana in a welter of conflicting emotions.

If she was honest with herself she could not regret letting Giacomo make love to her. It had been an experience transcending everything she had ever known or hoped to know. But it was an added complication.

She turned to look at him. The lines of his dark, ascetic profile were still relaxed in sleep. His jaw was dark-shadowed with an overnight growth of beard. Her gaze moved downwards over the male contours of his chest, finely coated with hair, down to that part of him that had given her so much pleasure.

Her heart began to thud and she was swept by a longing to know his lovemaking once more. Her lips parted on an involuntary shuddering inhalation of breath.

He must have been only on the final edge of sleep, for the slight sound was enough to wake him. He rolled on to his side and regarded her for a long quizzical moment.

'Still love me this morning, *cara mia*?'

There was no point now in denying it—she had given him only too adequate proof of her love last night. She nodded shyly, and his eyes widened and darkened with sensual awareness as they moved over her face and down to the naked creamy shoulders, the swell of her breasts rising and falling with increasing agitation.

'Sometimes it is as well to make up someone's mind for them,' he murmured tenderly as he reached out to pull her into his arms.

His kisses were slow and lazy at first, but Diana was in no

need of coaxing this morning. She was already on fire for him, an urgency in the pit of her stomach. But he took his time, exploring her mouth, pressing small kisses to her closed eyes, his tongue tracing the inner convolutions of her ear, his lips grazing on her neck as the waves of pulsating desire mounted within her.

Then as if he too could wait no longer he pinned her beneath him, his elemental urge matching hers, her soft, pliant body melded to his male hardness. On a shaken groan he murmured her name. Fierce pleasure burned inside her, and she revelled in the racing thud of his heart against hers as she gave herself up once more to his consuming desire.

'And now,' Giacomo said later—much later—'we must talk about our wedding day.'

'Our . . . our wedding day?'

'Of course.' He sounded amused. 'There is no point in waiting now. In fact it is essential we do not wait, in case you already carry my child.'

He was up and walking about the room with a restless energy, already making plans.

'We will send a message to your parents. You will give me their telephone number, *sì*? They will wish to be present? And to my cousin, the priest in Rome. He must marry us. And today we shall make the announcement public—at the *festa*.'

'*Festa*?' A bewildered Diana tried to follow the grasshopper leapings of his mind.

'*Sì*. It is an annual event. It is the anniversary day of my ancestor Rainulf Ortoni—without whom Solamenza would not exist. Up, up, *carissima*,' he urged her. 'It is late. Already the festivities will have been prepared.'

Diana made her way along the corridor to the nearest of

the hexagonal towers. Here, she had since discovered, was sited the bathroom whose unknown whereabouts had first led her into Giacomo Ortoni's bedroom.

She showered slowly, lethargically.

As always, away from Giacomo's compelling presence, she was assailed by anxieties. Once again events were moving too fast, carrying her with them on an inexorable tide. And she couldn't seem to think clearly.

But as the stinging cold water refreshed her, clearing her mind, one thought superseded all others. Giacomo had spoken of sending a message to her parents. What on earth would her family think when they learned she was to marry the Conte Ortoni—the man who everyone believed to be married to her cousin Julia? They would be horrified—worried too.

She had written to them once or twice from Florence, briefly outlining her lack of progress. She had written once only since she had been at Solamenza and they knew nothing of her intimacy with the Ortoni family, much less Giacomo himself.

And if her parents accepted Giacomo's invitation to Solamenza? She had given him their phone number. She could scarcely refuse. She would never be able to persuade them not to mention Julia. They would want their questions satisfactorily answered before they would accept their daughter's marriage. And it would all come out. Giacomo would know how she had deceived him.

'And let's face it,' she muttered to herself, 'in that case there won't *be* any wedding!' Though she loved Giacomo she had no illusions about his almost stiff-necked pride, his autocratic nature. He would be angry, and justifiably so.

So it was with very little heart herself for the festivities that she went to rouse Maria. She found the little girl sitting on the side of her bed, and at first the fact did not register as the child complained, 'Where is everyone? No one has been in with hot water. And I am hungry!'

'I expect they're all busy with the *festa*,' Diana said, and then, as it dawned on her, 'but if no one has been in to you, how did you get out of bed?'

'I suddenly found I could move.' Maria didn't sound as excited as Diana would have expected—or as excited as she herself felt.

'But how . . . ?'

'I wasn't thinking about it, I was just angry because no one came. But,' and the child's sensitive mouth quivered, 'I still can't walk. I stood up, but my legs wouldn't hold me, and I fell over.'

Diana flung her arms around her.

'That's not surprising,' she reassured her. 'Don't you see, darling, your legs are out of practice. They have to be made strong again. This is just a beginning.'

'Are you sure?' Maria asked doubtfully.

'I'm sure! And now we *must* tell your father. He will want you to have more physiotherapy.' Diana made as if to move away, but to her amazement Maria stopped her.

'No! Not yet. If you are right I want to practise first. I don't want him to know until I can get up and walk properly—I want to surprise him. I don't want the physiotherapist, I know all the exercises anyway. Will *you* help me, Diana?'

Throughout breakfast Diana and her charge exchanged gleeful conspiratorial glances. Fortunately everyone put it down to Giacomo's announcement that his marriage would take place very shortly.

'In a week's time, I hope, if my cousin is free to leave Rome.'

'Diana will want to go into Florence to purchase a trousseau,' Biella said excitedly.

Giacomo's 'No!' was sharp and decided. 'No one leaves Solamenza just now except me. Vitto and his friends are still active in their campaign against Sergio's reforms. Until the final reading of his bill next month no one is safe.'

'And what about when his bill is made law?' Diana put in. 'Won't things be just as bad? Won't your enemies want their revenge?'

'I hope Vitto's friends will be too busy saving their own skins to be after mine,' Giacomo said drily. 'Some of them already face conviction and stiff sentences if they can be apprehended.'

'And Vitto himself?' Diana pressed anxiously.

'Without his minions,' Giacomo assured her, 'the sting will be drawn from the viper's tail.' Scornfully, 'Alone, Vitto is a man of straw.'

'L-like me!' Stefano put in with sudden bitterness, drawing everyone's attention.

'Nonsense!' Faustina said at once with severe briskness. 'The cases are quite unalike.' And with tactless bluntness, 'He has not the excuse of poor health for his weak nature.'

'What m-my aunt means,' Stefano told Diana wryly, 'is m-mental health. I had a nervous b-breakdown, when . . .'

'That is no discredit to you,' Giacomo interrupted him. 'The blame for that lies on other shoulders. And now . . .' with a determined change of subject, 'for the *festa*. The people will be wondering why their *padrone* and his family are late. Fortunately,' he smiled knowingly at Diana, making her blush, 'he has the best of reasons!'

Considering no motor traffic could reach the central *piazza* of Solamenza, the town presented a busy scene. Stalls had been set up offering all kinds of wares—the products of local home industries, as well as brilliant tawdries and charms against *malocchio*, the evil eye.

'But who will buy all this?' marvelled Diana. 'Surely they don't all buy from each other?'

'Today Solamenza opens its gates to the nearby villages,' Giacomo told her.

Cries of '*L'Aquila*!' followed by cheers greeted thc arrival of the Conte and his party. Diana watched Giacomo with loving pride as he mounted a small decorated rostrum to make his traditional speech of opening, his olive-skinned good looks enhanced by the simple black shirt and trousers he wore. In a few well chosen words, he lauded Rainulf, his illustrious forebear, and invited his people to make merry.

'And today,' he went on, still speaking in his own tongue, but Diana had no difficulty in following his words, 'we have even greater cause for rejoicing. Today I announce my forthcoming marriage—to the English *signorina*. Diana!' He turned and beckoned to her to join him on the platform. Shyly she did so, going into the circle of his arm as he introduced her to the people of Solamenza.

There was more applause and cries of congratulation, then Giacomo declared the *festa* 'open'. The town band struck up a lively march, and as though that were a signal, a procession appeared, led by men carrying statues of saints and pagan symbols with a quaint disregard for the incongruity of religion and superstition.

Some of the more exalted among the townsfolk surged forward, surrounding Diana, shaking her hand.

'You must have your fortune told,' an elderly man with skin like a lizard advised her. 'To see what the future holds for you and *L'Aquila* . . .' and, making the ready colour run up under her skin, 'many *bambinos, si*?'

'And now,' Giacomo told her when he had succeeded in dragging her away from the well-wishers, 'we must patronise all the stalls. It is expected.'

Obediently Diana purchased a few trinkets as well as some of the lace produced by the industrious townswomen. And Giacomo bought her one of the charms against the evil eye.

'Now you are doubly protected against ill fortune,' he joked as he hung it around her neck together with her own lucky black cat.

Diana shivered, as a superstitious sense of foreboding reminded her of the difficulties still to be surmounted in her relationship with Giacomo Ortoni.

Having made a token appearance, the elderly aunts and uncles retreated into the castle, and Diana noticed that Stefano too did not remain long. But, hand in hand, she and Giacomo mingled with the noisy, happy crowd, trying their hand at sideshows and watching the entertainers. But for the different language and the blazing heat of the sun, they might have been an English milord and his wife patronising a village fête.

'Goodness!' Diana exclaimed as one circle of onlookers parted to allow their *padrone* through. 'Is that a *real* snake?'

'*Si*. The *serpari*—snake-charmers—of the Abruzzi are famous.'

Diana gazed in repelled fascination as a youth allowed the large yellow snake to coil around him. Its evil-looking narrow head moved rhythmically from side to side in the motion supposed to hypnotise its victims. As part of his act the young man moved around the inner perimeter of the crowd, draping his snake around the shoulders of certain members of his audience.

'Can we move on?' Diana asked Giacomo as the

performer drew nearer to where they stood.

'You do not care for snakes?' Giacomo guessed, and as she agreed vehemently, 'But it is considered good luck to wear the snake. Are you not eager for good fortune?'

Her superstitions thus appealed to, Diana braced herself for the unpleasant experience. But when the snake was actually placed across Giacomo's shoulders and her own she found it less traumatic than she had supposed. She had never touched a snake's skin before, and instead of finding it moist and slimy as she had expected, it was warm and dry to the touch.

The *serparo* said something she did not quite catch and she looked at Giacomo for a translation.

'He says we are now inextricably linked by fate. But we knew that already, did we not, *cara mia*?' His green eyes were tenderly possessive.

They moved on to a fortune-teller's booth, Giacomo insisting that without this Diana's day would not be complete.

To her consternation she discovered the fortune-teller was none other than Assunta, suitably dressed for the occasion and with a gaudy parrot perched on her shoulder.

'Como, I . . . I don't think . . .' she began, but Giacomo had already paid the small fee.

At a word from Assunta, the parrot—whose purpose Diana had wondered at—climbed on to its owner's finger. It fixed Diana with an eye no less baleful than Assunta's, then from a container selected a small folded slip of paper.

'This is known as divination by *sortes*,' Giacomo explained in a low voice. 'It was a system much used in ancient Greece or Rome. In those days the diviner was usually a child—not a parrot.'

Gingerly Diana took the paper from the parrot's beak and

while Assunta rewarded the bird with a handful of seeds, she read her future, Giacomo looking over her shoulder.

'Beware a man in black,' the words read, 'he brings trouble.'

Giacomo laughed.

'It seems you are to beware of *me, carissima,*' he indicated his dark clothing. 'The gipsy's warning comes a little late, I fear.'

'Como!' Diana set an urgent hand on his arm as they emerged from the stuffy confines of the booth.

He looked down at her, arrested by something in her tone of voice.

'What is it, *cara mia?*'

'Please,' she besought him earnestly, 'whatever happens, don't stop loving me.'

Giacomo covered her hand with his own and regarded her thoughtfully.

'What *should* happen?' he asked, and as she did not, could not, reply, 'You really do take these things to heart? But it is only a diversion—an entertaining nonsense. You cannot really believe harm will come to you through me?' He laughed a little. 'If I did not know it was impossible, I would almost suspect Assunta of "fixing" that fortune.'

'Do you think she'll ever accept me?' asked Diana with a sigh as they strolled back towards the castle.

'*Si,*' he said with a comforting pressure of her hand. 'Give her time. She is old, and the old adapt slowly. By the way,' he went on, 'I telephoned to Rome early this morning before you were up. My cousin the priest was not available, but I have left a message.'

'Did you . . . ?' She hardly dared to ask. 'Did you phone England too?'

'It was not possible to obtain a connection. I shall try

again this evening when the lines are less busy.' He looked at her downcast face. 'You *do* wish your parents to attend our wedding? You are not afraid they will disapprove?'

If Giacomo believed her parents likely to dissuade her, Diana thought, he might—in his autocratic way—decide to marry her out of hand. At least that way she might not have to tell her family about her marriage until the question of Julia was settled. She'd given a lot of thought to the problem in the last few hours and she had come to a decision.

Ever since the night when Faustina had found Giacomo in Diana's bedroom, Diana had been certain the elderly woman knew something about Julia. And it seemed likely that what Faustina knew, Biella would know too. And Biella loved to gossip.

Besides, now that Diana was to marry her great-nephew, surely there would be no need for the secrecy which Giacomo—according to Faustina—had imposed on his family. Diana knew Biella was fond of her, and even Faustina had unbent a little since, under Diana's influence, Maria had begun to talk again.

If she could just get Biella on her own, Diana was sure she could lead the subject round to Maria's former companions and thus to Julia. It was worth a try.

'Diana?' Giacomo's voice recalled her. 'You seem suddenly very *distraite*. *Will* your parents disapprove? Is that what is troubling you?'

'Aye, they . . . they might do.'

But she had reckoned without Giacomo's sense of what was due to one's family.

'Then,' he said with cheerful confidence, 'we shall just have to persuade them that I am a fitting husband for you. I shall invite them here immediately, so that they may get to know me before the wedding takes place.'

To Diana's relief, Giacomo was still unable to obtain his telephone connection. It was possible her parents were away; they sometimes did take a break about this time of year. But the reprieve could only be a short one. Which made it all the more imperative that she speak to Biella. But before the conversation could take place, fate took a hand.

Diana spent most of the next morning with Maria, helping the child with her exercises and encouraging her to try out her still shaky legs. Things were progressing well and Diana felt certain that before long they would be able to surprise Giacomo as Maria planned.

Leaving Maria to rest after her exertions, she went downstairs, bent on cornering Biella. She found the family gathered in the main *salone*. There was a newcomer in their midst. His back was towards her, but he wore the black garb of a priest, and with a sudden fluttering of her nerves Diana guessed that this must be the cousin from Rome. His arrival brought the wedding ceremony that much closer. Time was running out.

'Diana, *carissima*!' Giacomo had caught sight of her. 'Come and be introduced to my cousin, Padre Ortoni. Ottavio, this is my betrothed, Signorina Diana Watt.'

The priest turned towards her. He was of medium height, gaunt with iron-grey hair, and he was vaguely familiar. As Diana held out her hand to him she saw the green eyes that she had come to associate with the Ortoni family grow narrow and cold. Slowly a dull shade of purple crept up the priest's thin throat. He ignored her outstretched hand and with a sudden movement grasped Giacomo's elbow, turning him away, steering him to the other side of the room, talking all the while in a swift, vehement undertone.

Hurt and puzzled by his obvious rejection of her, Diana

watched and saw the gradual darkening of Giacomo's face. Several times he darted glances in her direction and she saw his expression change from one of horrified incredulity to that of black fury.

The rest of the family seemed as taken aback as Diana herself, exchanging questioning looks among themselves. Finally Giacomo spoke.

'Diana, you will oblige me by accompanying us to my study.' His voice was harsh. He used none of his usual endearments. He had become an angry stranger.

On shaking legs, Diana followed as Giacomo and his cousin led the way. In the study Giacomo took up his stance below his portrait, and it seemed to her that both the man and his likeness accused her.

'*You*,' he told her, 'have a lot of explaining to do. While *I*, it seems, have been a gullible fool—your dupe. Oh, but my enemies chose their weapon very cleverly this time!'

'Your . . . your enemies?' she stammered. 'But I . . .'

'It is useless to deny it. Ottavio has told me everything.'

'What can *he* possibly know about me?' she demanded indignantly. 'He only met me for the first time today . . . d-didn't he?' Her voice quavered as doubt set in and again she had a sense that the priest's face was familiar to her.

'It is just unfortunate for you,' Giacomo told her, 'that Ottavio's ministry takes him into the haunts of criminals, of thieves and . . .' he paused, then with great significance '. . . and of *prostitutes*.'

Diana gasped. Of course! The house of Elsa Ortoni. That was where she'd seen him. The priest who had come to give the Holy Week blessing. But surely he didn't think . . . She'd told him she wasn't . . . Giacomo couldn't believe . . . ?

'I'm not a prostitute!' she declared fiercely. 'And if your cousin has told you I am then he's a liar!'

'He has not accused you of any such thing,' Giacomo snapped. 'But the name you gave Ottavio,' he snapped, 'is not the name you gave me. Is *either* name the correct one? And what *were* you doing at the *bordello* of my cousin Vitto?'

'Vitto!' Diana exclaimed. Light was beginning to dawn.

'I am glad you do not pretend the name is unfamiliar to you,' Giacomo said without a trace of gladness in his manner.

A jigsaw of seemingly unconnected pieces was coming together in Diana's head. Elsa's wealthy *protettore*. Minister Sergio Ortoni's battle against immorality.

'I've never met Vitto Ortoni,' she began. 'I only . . .'

'Spare me any more lies, the look of injured innocence,' Giacomo sneered. 'It would look well, would it not, for my uncle Sergio's campaign if his nephew the Conte of Solamenza had taken one of Vitto's agents as his wife? You are not the first woman he has sent here in this way. Vitto, the very man Sergio seeks to overthrow!'

'I am *not* . . .' an outraged Diana began.

'But then marriage was not necessarily your target, was it, Diana?' he went on inexorably. 'No wonder you were so coy about naming a day! The mere association of our names would be enough—the fact that we had slept together. Oh yes, Ottavio . . .' Now Giacomo addressed the priest, who had drawn in a horrified breath, '*mea culpa*—but then I thought she would be my bride in a few days. How could I guess that anyone so apparently lovely—her nature, it seemed, as well as her appearance—was a liar, a cheat—another infiltrator.'

'Como, please!' Diana's voice broke on a sob and she moved towards him, hands outstretched. 'Listen to me. It's not what you . . .'

'No wonder you had no references to give me!' Giacomo retreated behind his desk as though any contact with her would contaminate him. 'And I in my foolishness trusted your word that you had sent for them. And no wonder you got on so well with Tomaso! How successfully you held my attention elsewhere while he made his attempt on Maria! How chagrined you must have felt at his failure.'

'I love Maria,' Diana choked, 'I wouldn't harm her. I wanted to help her—I *have* helped her. Oh, Como, please, please let me speak to you alone, so that I can . . .'

'So that you can beguile him with your female wiles.' It was the priest who spoke this time, sternly condemnatory. 'Have you and your friend Vitto not caused enough harm? I trust you are not a Catholic? For the way you lied to me, a minister of God, would lie heavily on your soul.'

'Beware a man in black.' The fortune-teller's warning flashed through Diana's mind and she rounded on the priest.

'*I* haven't caused *anyone* any harm. Como's enemies are *not* my friends. I *told* you why I was at Elsa Ortoni's. It's all a misunderstanding, which I could put straight if only you'd let me get a word in.'

But her impassioned outburst was ignored.

'It is as well that Giacomo is made of sterner stuff than his brother,' the priest went on grimly. 'The other Englishwoman reduced Stefano to a nervous breakdown.' He turned to his cousin. 'It had not occurred to me that the names were the same. But then why should it? I had no idea that this woman sought you. She spoke only of a cousin.'

The other Englishwoman! Diana abandoned caution. Right now there was no way these stern-faced men were going to listen to her story. Perhaps later, when his immediate anger had cooled, she might be able to appeal to

Giacomo's reason, to his sense of fair play. At least she deserved a hearing. But for now she might as well be hanged for a sheep as a lamb.

'The other Englishwoman?' she asked. 'You obviously *do* mean Julia McWinter? What's happened to her? As you've rightly guessed, *she's* my cousin.'

The two men exchanged glances.

'As I suspected, the bad blood runs in the family,' said Ottavio. 'Como, my cousin, you have had a lucky escape.'

'What do you mean, bad blood?' Diana demanded. 'Neither my cousin nor I are . . . anyway, we're not blood relations. My uncle and aunt adopted her as a baby.'

'You both came from Vitto, did you not? You both sought to deceive me.' Giacomo's voice was shaking with anger. 'If it is not in the blood it is in the character—and *you* spoke of bearing me children!' At his sides his hands balled into fists. 'Thank God that was just one of your ploys! If I believed you bore my child I think I would kill you. But no, you were protected against that, weren't you?' He laughed sardonically. 'And to think I apologised to you for the risk I had taken!'

'Where *is* my cousin?' Diana managed to persist, though her lips trembled and she was afraid she would burst into tears.

'Julia,' Giacomo said, 'is in hospital in Florence.'

'A hospital endowed by my cousin,' the priest put in grimly. 'He is generous even to his enemies. What have you to say to that?' Don Ottavio demanded. Diana's dislike for her austere accuser was growing rapidly. Yet, when she had met him in Rome, she had thought him a kindly man.

'What's wrong with Julia? She's the reason I came to Italy in the first place—to try and find her, because her letters stopped, because she seemed to have disappeared and all we

knew was that she had become involved with a Conte
Ortoni. Her mother—my aunt—was worried . . . I *dared* not
give Como my real name, in case he was responsible for her
disappearance.'

'Lies,' the priest said scornfully, 'more lies.'

'*I am not lying*!' Diana told him vehemently. Anger gave
her the courage to hold his condemning gaze. 'Why should
I have lied to *you*?' she demanded triumphantly, 'when I
had no idea who you were—that you were an Ortoni?'

The priest was scornful again.

'You expect me to believe that Elsa had not boasted of the
connection?'

'I *did* tell *you* my real name,' Diana pointed out, and
Giacomo turned to his cousin.

'This could be true,' he said. There was a note of hope in
his voice. But at once the priest destroyed it.

'Como, do not allow this woman to bewitch you again. If
you are sensible you will send her away today, now. Even so
it may be too late.' And as his cousin looked at him
questioningly: 'Yesterday was a *festa* in Solamenza. The
castle gates were thrown open to all. Who knows whether
the Roman *paparazzi* were there, tipped off by Vitto, taking
photographs of you with this woman? In a few days Sergio's
Immorality Bill will be voted on. A story such as this in the
Roman newspapers—connecting you with an agent from
Vitto—could ruin everything.'

Giacomo's face was haggard. For a long, agonising
moment he stared into Diana's eyes, then he nodded.

'You are right, Ottavio. She must leave. Attend to it for
me, will you? He turned away as if he could no longer bear
to look at Diana. He pressed a bell behind his desk. 'I do
not wish to see or speak to her again.'

'Como,' Diana spoke his name imploringly, took a few

steps towards him, 'if you'd only give me a chance! If you'd only listen to me for ten minutes without interrupting . . .'

'Enough!' Sternly the priest cut across her plea, interposing his gaunt body between her and Giacomo, and as he did so the door opened, admitting Luca and Ubaldo.

'Escort the *padre* and . . . and this woman back to Rome,' Giacomo commanded, 'and do not take your eyes off her until she is on an aeroplane for England.'

With a bodyguard on either side, holding her arms in no gentle grip, and the priest hard upon her heels, Diana made one last desperate appeal.

'Como, go to Elsa Ortoni. Ask her what I was doing in her house. Ask Nigel Lambert at the British Embassy in Rome. I don't know what Julia got up to or whether she had anything to do with your enemies, but *I* had nothing to do with them, with their plots, I swear it!'

Then she was hustled from the room, her last sight of Giacomo his stern averted profile.

CHAPTER EIGHT

'I WOULD have thought you'd have had enough of Italy, the Italians and the Ortonis in particular!'

Once again Diana was in the busy noise-filled departure lounge at Heathrow with her friend Susan and a party of tourists.

'And I'm surprised His Nibs is letting you go back to Italy after the way you practically disappeared there last time.'

'Don't you see, I *have* to go back,' Diana explained. There was a hint of desperation in her soft Scottish voice.

'Surely you're not going to try and see Giacomo Ortoni, not after the way he and his family treated you?'

'I would if I thought it would do any good,' sighed Diana. 'But I don't suppose I'd be allowed to get anywhere near Como. No, I'm going back because I still have to find Julia. And the fact that this tour is going to Florence is heaven-sent. You'll cover for me if I slip away from the party for a few hours, won't you, Sue?'

'Of course,' her friend said loyally. 'But do be careful, Di,' she worried. 'Suppose you get kidnapped by the *bad* Ortonis this time? Whatever would I tell your family? Do your parents know what happened and what you're up to this time?'

'Och, no. No need to upset Auntie Marion until we know the whole truth. I telephoned them when I got back from Rome the other day. Just to say I thought I was on Julia's trail at last.' Diana's attractive face darkened. 'I begged Don Ottavio to let me stop off in Florence to see Julia, but he was so determined to have me out of the country . . .'

'Do you believe this story about Julia's illness? Suppose Giacomo *is* a bad lot too?'

'He's not,' Diana said, 'I'm sure of it.' Her blue eyes became wistful and her soft mouth drooped. Her heartache had grown with every day away from him. 'I believe he's a very good man. He does a lot of charitable work. His people and his family adore him and . . . I love him, Sue. And aye, I do believe it may be true what he said about Julia. But I got the idea that it wasn't so much that Julia was ill, but that there'd been an accident of some kind.'

'Something that happened in Italy!' Susan exclaimed, 'but that still means the Ortonis could have caused it. Diana, *you* could get hurt again. Suppose you're wrong about Giacomo? Suppose you find out . . . ?'

'It's a risk I have to take. And anyway,' Diana said courageously, 'surely it's better that I should know the truth? If I'm wrong about Giacomo it would make it a lot easier to forget about him.' But despite her brave words she knew she would never forget Giacomo Ortoni. Some day perhaps it might not hurt as much, but she would never love any man as she still loved him.

It was strange to be back in picturesque Florence, the city now as familiar to her as her own home and indelibly coloured by memories of her time there with Giacomo.

It was surprisingly easy to find the hospital endowed by the Conte Ortoni. It seemed even the ordinary person in the street had heard of him and his generosity.

'*Si*! *Buon uomo. Forte e gentile!*' her informant told her enthusiastically, and with almost embarrassing courtesy insisted on accompanying her to the very doors of the white modern building.

Nor did she encounter any difficulty within the hospital walls.

'A relation of Signorina McWinter!' the attractive dark-eyed nurse exclaimed. 'After a year we had given up hope of finding her relations.'

'Didn't she have any papers on her?' asked Diana, 'her passport, her address?'

'Nothing,' the nurse said as she escorted Diana into a little office, where, she explained, one of the doctors would presently see her. 'Your cousin has been well looked after,' she assured Diana, and she too sang Giacomo Ortoni's praises. 'He has been most regular in his visits to the poor lady. Her medical expenses have all been charged to him.'

Dr Genaro, who had been attending Julia throughout her illness, had encouragement to offer.

'It is true the *signorina* has been very ill,' he told Diana in his impeccable though heavily accented English. 'It is a wonder she was not killed. As it is, she sustained several broken ribs and severe facial injuries. There has been much plastic surgery—all paid for by the Conte. And she is also suffering from amnesia—she has been unable to tell us anything about herself. Your arrival is most opportune. Perhaps the sight of a familiar face . . . a member of her family . . .'

'Will I be able to take her back to England?' asked Diana.

'I would not recommend it at present. Perhaps in a few weeks and then in the charge of a medical attendant. She will need more operations. I would ask you not to tire her. She still needs plenty of rest.'

Julia was in a cheerful private room provided with every comfort. In appearance, Diana found her cousin very much

changed—if not as hideously deformed as she had
feared—though certainly surgery had achieved wonders, if
the doctor's account of her injuries were to be believed.
And in manner she was very different too. She had been a
restless, energetic child, highly strung and volatile. Now
she seemed lethargic and withdrawn. At the sight of Diana
and Doctor Genaro her expression did not change.

'Now, Signorina McWinter,' Doctor Genaro said
cheerfully, 'here is your cousin come to visit you.' And
when this did not elicit any response, he told Diana, 'I will
leave you alone with her. Talk to her, remind her of her
home and family—it may help. But not for too long, please.'

With the doctor's departure Diana sat down by her
cousin's bed. Unaccustomed to illness, she was at rather a
loss where to begin.

'Hello, Julia,' she said. 'I'm glad I've found you.'

'Are you?' To Diana's amazement the answer came
promptly and cynically. 'Why? There was never any love
lost between us.' And as Diana, totally at a loss for words,
gaped at her. 'Oh, I know what's going on—*now*. I admit
there seem to be a few months missing out of my life. But
I've known who I am and where I am for a week or two
now. I listen to them talking about me, you know. It's quite
amusing.'

'But why haven't you let them know how much better
you are?'

'Look around you,' Julia drawled. It was part of her
snobbery that she had entirely eradicated her Scottish
accent. 'Would you exchange all this for an English
National Health hospital? Besides, I reckon the Ortoni
family owe me.'

Diana felt excitement welling within her. If she handled
Julia carefully, not betraying her own intense

involvement—for Julia wouldn't accord *her* any favours—she stood a good chance of finding out the story of her cousin's involvement with the Ortonis.

'Auntie Marion's been very worried about you. She asked me to try and find you. The last she heard you were supposed to be getting married to someone called Ortoni.'

Julia's face darkened.

'The lying swine!'

'Who?'

'Vitto Ortoni.'

Diana drew in a breath of relief. At first she'd thought her cousin was referring to Giacomo.

'What happened?'

'I met Vitto at a nightclub in Rome. He was incredibly handsome—black hair, green eyes, olive-skinned. You can imagine the sort of thing.'

Knowing Giacomo Ortoni and guessing there must be a strong family likeness, Diana certainly could imagine it.

Julia yawned profusely. 'Damn this everlasting tiredness! Well, I fell for Vitto like a ton of bricks,' she went on. 'He told me he came from a noble family. He didn't use his title, he said, but he was actually entitled to call himself Count Ortoni.'

'And that was a lie?' Diana asked carefully.

'It was his distant cousin who was the real count. But I didn't find that out until later, much later. Vitto had it in for this cousin and another member of his family, some Government Minister—he didn't tell me the full story. But he asked me to help him put one over on them. I was crazy about Vitto—I thought he meant it when he said he wanted to marry me—so I agreed.'

'What did he ask you to do?' asked Diana when, momentarily, Julia seemed to withdraw to some secret inner place of recollection.

Julia yawned again. 'He wanted me to pose as an *au pair*, sent by an agency in Rome. Vitto got me forged references—I suppose that should have told me the sort he was. I should have been suspicious too when he told me to leave my passport and all other documents with him. But I was too besotted. Anyway, he wanted me inside his cousin's household looking after his crippled daughter. He and his sister Iolanda introduced me to another cousin, Stefano, Como's brother. They told me to make up to Stefano, let him think I fancied him. As double insurance for getting into the household.'

'What were you supposed to do there?' Diana prompted as again Julia fell silent.

'I thought I was just there as some kind of spy. He said he wanted to get some dirt on his cousin. I didn't know at first that he was planning to kidnap the daughter. And she wasn't bad as kids go.'

'Would you have helped him do that?'

'I might have done,' said Julia, '*before* I met Como Ortoni. Boy! I thought Vitto Ortoni was handsome, but Como . . . now he was really something. But,' viciously, 'I hate him now. I like seeing him suffer. That's another reason I don't mind staying here.' She gave a bitter laugh. '*He* feels it's his duty to visit me every week.' She lay back against the pillows, closing her eyes, as though the vituperation had exhausted her.

'Julia?' Diana prompted gently.

'Hmm?' With an obvious effort, Julia's eyes opened again. 'Oh, well, when I found out Vitto wasn't a count at all I thought why not go for the genuine article? Como Ortoni was a widower. There didn't seem to be any other women in his life.'

'So you played up to *him*? And what about Stefano?'

'He was a real wet fish,' Julia said in scornful dismissal. 'You wouldn't think he had the same blood in him. I bet no woman had ever looked at him before. I really must have bowled him over, because he made a real fuss when I stopped paying him attention. Said he was in love with me, that he couldn't live without me. Even threatened to kill himself.'

'And Giacomo Ortoni?' Diana's heart was thudding erratically.

'I thought I had it made there—at first. He was charm itself,' Julia said reminiscently. 'He was friendly—very friendly. I thought he fancied me too. I forgot all about Vitto. Well, there was no comparison. And Como had the title and the money—all that I'd ever wanted. But that was as far as it seemed to go. I couldn't understand it—most of the Italians I'd met were real fast movers. So I thought I'd help him along a bit.' Her face darkened.

'And?'

'He went all moral and righteous on me. Said he was sorry if he'd given me the wrong impression and I'd misunderstood his friendliness but · he just wasn't interested, etc., etc. Damn him! Diana,' Julia's voice broke. 'It wasn't like it was with Vitto. I was really in love with Como. And then he said it would be best for everyone if I left. That really broke me up. I begged and pleaded with him not to send me away—just to be near him would have been enough. But he was adamant. I shouted at him then, screamed, told him I hoped he got his come-uppance. Stupidly I must have said something about Vitto—I don't really remember. Anyway, I rushed out of the *palazzo*. I took one of his cars. One of his men came after me in the other car. I wasn't used to driving on the right. I crashed—and the rest I suppose you know. When I came to . . .' Julia shuddered and slumped back against her pillows, 'I couldn't remember a thing. It was horrible. And,' her voice quivered, 'they wouldn't give me a mirror. I wanted to see if I recognised myself. I'm ugly now, aren't I, Diana? Ugly!'

'No,' Diana said quickly. Despite their childhood antagonism and Julia's behaviour while in Italy, compassion welled up inside her for her adopted cousin. 'They've done a marvellous job on your face—honestly, Julia. In a few more months no one will ever know. But wouldn't you rather come home now that I've found you?' she coaxed gently. 'To your own family? Staying here can only remind you . . .' But Julia wasn't listening. Exhaustion had claimed her once more. And, belatedly, Diana remembered the doctor's injunction not to tire her cousin.

'Frankly, *signorina*,' Dr Genaro said when Diana rejoined him in his office, 'as long as the Conte is willing for her to stay here at his expense it would be best if she remained until her treatment is completed. From what you tell me, her mother is practically an invalid. She could not care for her daughter at home. Besides, more operations are necessary, and as Signorina McWinter said, she would only exchange one hospital for another.'

'Aye, perhaps you're right,' Diana agreed. 'But that's a decision I shall have to leave to my aunt.' She got up to leave, holding out her hand. 'Thank you for your help, Dr Genaro.'

'But you are not leaving yet?' the doctor queried.

'I must. I'm in Florence because of my work. I have a party of holidaymakers . . .'

'No, please,' the doctor seemed quite perturbed. 'I must ask you to remain a little longer. Conte Ortoni . . .'

'What about him?' Diana demanded sharply. At the sound of Giacomo's name her stomach seemed to turn a triple somersault.

'I telephoned the Conte, to tell him a relative of Signorina Julia had at last come to claim her. Until now we had no details about her. He is on his way here. He wishes to see you.'

'Oh, no!' Diana knew she must have gone white, from the way the doctor hurried around the table and pressed his own glass of water into her hand.

'*Signorina*, there is no need for alarm. He is the kindest of men. You will like him.'

'It's not that . . .' She struggled to rise. 'I can't . . . I don't want to see him. Please, you must let me go before he gets here!'

Dr Genaro was even more worried. He even stood between Diana and the door.

'The Conte is my patron. His money runs this hospital. I cannot offend him.'

'You can tell him it wasn't your fault. You couldn't stop me. You tried, but I . . .' The rest of the words died on Diana's lips as the door behind the doctor opened and Giacomo Ortoni strode into the little office, dominating it, filling it with his presence.

'Diana!'

She had never expected to hear him say her name again or meet the gaze of those startling green eyes. He turned to the doctor.

'My deepest gratitude, Genaro.'

'You wish to use my office for your interview with the *signorina*?'

'No. Thank you, but no. What I have to say to Signorina McWinter will take some considerable time. I shall not inconvenience you.'

To the sound of the doctor's polite denials Giacomo grasped Diana's elbow and swept her from the room. He was moving so fast that she had to run to keep up and her legs trembled beneath her.

'You needn't think you're hustling me out of Italy again,' she told him defiantly as he hurried her along the corridors redolent of disinfectant and other typical hospital smells. 'I'm here because of my work. My *real* work,' she emphasised as he didn't answer. 'I work for a travel firm. There are people depending on me.'

Outside the hospital stood a familiar limousine, and Diana tried to hang back as Giacomo urged her towards it.

'Far from sending you away, Diana, I intend to make sure that you never leave Italy again.'

'What do you mean?' She tried once more to wrench her arm free. Was he planning to lock her up somewhere? 'I didn't come back meaning to cause you any embarrassment,' she assured him. 'I only wanted to find my cousin.'

'I know, I know,' he said soothingly. 'But we cannot talk here—I am illegally parked, for one thing. Please, Diana, *cara mia*, trust me, hmm?'

Perhaps it was the sound of the endearment on his lips, something she had thought never to hear again. Afterwards she couldn't decide. But somehow she was in the limousine and Giacomo was driving rapidly through the busy narrow streets.

'It is a wonder I was not arrested on my way here,' he told her with a glint of humour in his eyes. But Diana was not feeling amused.

'Where are you taking me?' she demanded.

'To the *palazzo*, of course. Where else? It was fortunate

that it was my day for visiting Florence. I would have been coming to the hospital later in any case. Thank heavens Genaro had the sense to telephone and tell me you were there. To think I might have missed you!'

Diana ventured a sideways glance at him. It had almost sounded as though that would have been a tragedy. But even so, 'I warn you, my family and friends know where I am,' she told him.

The large iron gates to the *palazzo* stood open and there was no sign of any brawny bodyguards.

'There is no longer any need,' Giacomo told her in answer to her question. 'In the last week Sergio's reforms have gone through. But in any case, Vitto and his associates have been arrested for their varied crimes. Our branch of the Ortoni family may now come and go without fear.'

'What about Iolanda?' asked Diana as they entered the *palazzo*.

'Ah, of course, you met Vitto's sister.' Now how did Giacomo know that? 'Though she was loyal to her brother she was not actually involved in any of his criminal activities. She is free to go on with her life.'

They were in the well-remembered *salone* now, with its priceless furnishings and treasures—and the portraits that had been Diana's first introduction to the Ortoni good looks. Giacomo motioned her to a seat. He, however, seemed too restless to sit down but moved about the apartment. Hungrily, Diana watched him, relearning every detail of those dark attractive features.

'What did you think of your cousin?' he asked.

Diana sighed.

'I couldn't help feeling sorry for her, however stupidly she may have behaved. I feel sorry for my aunt too—it's going to be an awful shock to her. But perhaps she'll be so

relieved Julia's alive . . .' She hesitated, then, 'Thank you
for all you've done for Julia. It was good of you after the
way she planned to . . . to deceive you.' Her voice faltered
away and she could not meet his eyes. She'd deceived
Giacomo too. Would she also receive kindness at his hands?

'My anger was chiefly against Vitto,' said Giacomo. 'Julia
was merely a tool in his hands—as I thought you were.' He
used the past tense, and Diana felt hope well up inside her.
She looked up quickly. But Giacomo was still pacing the
room, still speaking. 'I was angry too at her treatment of
Stefano—again at Vitto's instigation. My brother is not of a
strong character. Her rejection of him was bad enough. But
when she was nearly killed in that accident, it was too much
for his fragile nerves. He suffered a most severe nervous
breakdown, from which he is only just recovering.'

'Poor Stefano,' murmured Diana. 'Is that why you
forbade anyone to talk about Julia?'

'*Si*. But for Maria's sake too. Her afflictions stemmed
from the time of her mother's death, and she had grown
attached to Julia. I did not want her to have any more
shocks.'

And Maria had thought her father implicated in some
sinister way in Julia's disappearance! Giacomo was much to
be pitied too, and Diana's blue eyes were eloquent as she
looked up at him.

'You said you *thought* I was sent here by Vitto. Do you
still believe that?' She waited breathlessly for his answer.

'No. I *know* you were not.' He sighed and began to toy
with a costly piece of china, turning it over and over in his
shapely hands, not looking at her. 'Diana, can you ever
forgive me for my unworthy suspicions?'

'They weren't unworthy,' she contradicted him. 'They
were perfectly justified. I *had* deceived you about some

things. All the evidence was against me.'

'Nevertheless I should have given you a hearing.' He set the china down with a bang and she almost expected to see it shatter. 'If it had not been for Ottavio's presence . . .'

'Och, him!' Diana exclaimed. 'He . . .'

'No,' Giacomo interrupted her, 'do not be too hard on Ottavio. He is stern in matters of morals and religion. But he is also a man of conscience. He has more than made amends for his suspicions of you.'

'How?'

Giacomo stopped his pacing and stood looking down at her.

'When you left Solamenza you begged me to go to Elsa Ortoni, also to see some young man at the British Embassy. Somehow, when my anger had cooled a little, the more I thought about your denials, about what I had learned of you, the more I began to wonder if I had misjudged you.' His voice grew husky. 'I could not believe it possible that I could feel such a deep love for a woman of unscrupulous character.'

'Oh, Como!' Diana said softly, and for a moment she thought he would move towards her. But he resumed his pacing.

'I telephoned Ottavio, I told him my feelings. I told him I meant to do as you asked, to visit these people. But he would not hear of it.'

'He forbade you to go?' she queried. 'Why, the . . .'

'No . . . hear me out.' Again Giacomo came to a halt. This time he was close enough to where she sat for her to be able to inhale the subtle aroma of his presence. She clenched her hands in her lap, forcing herself to concentrate instead on what he was saying. 'Ottavio reminded me of Elsa Ortoni's occupation. He said it would give rise to the scandal we had tried to avoid if I were seen going there. Whereas *he*—for the sake of his ministry—was a regular visitor. At that time he was still unconvinced of your innocence, but torn by the recollection that initially he had liked you. So for my sake he agreed to make enquiries.'

'And?' Diana was trembling, but not from any fear of what he would say. She *knew* she was innocent. She was trembling because, almost imperceptibly, Giacomo had drawn closer and she could sense a new kind of restlessness in him now, a restlessness that matched her own inner flutterings.

'Elsa confirmed that the "Englishwoman" had been in her house purely by chance—an act of charity on Elsa's part following a street accident. Since Elsa did not know of the suspicions linking you to Vitto, she had no reason to tell anything but the truth.'

'Thank heavens!' Diana exclaimed.

'But Ottavio did not stop there. He went to the Embassy, and there he heard the full story of your search for your cousin, that you had been given Elsa Ortoni's address, as well as that of Iolanda.'

'When . . . when did he tell you all this?'

'I only learned the full story yesterday. Diana.' His hand made a movement towards her and then withdrew. 'Diana, I swear to you, if you had not come back to Florence, I was coming in search of you. I had booked a flight for tomorrow. I don't know England, or Scotland, but somehow I would have found you.'

Diana's pulses were skittering wildly. His body was throwing out a powerful sexual stimulant. The whole room was filled with an atmosphere of sensual tension that was triggering off a reaction that made her body ache.

'Why, Como?' she asked huskily. 'Why would you have

come looking for me?'

'To apologise, of course,' he said, and her heart sank again. 'To apologise for my doubts of you, for the terrible accusations I hurled at you. To ask your forgiveness.' He stopped, looking down at the bowed golden head. 'Would you have forgiven me, Diana? *Do* you forgive me?'

'Of course,' she lifted her head and forced herself to say it brightly. 'If I had gone about things honestly in the first place—asked you straight out about Julia . . .'

'You did what you thought was best,' he said softly. 'And in one sense it has proved a blessing. A simple enquiry and you would have been on your way.' He was only a hair's breadth away from her now and Diana had to make a tremendous effort to stop herself trembling. Giacomo might have wanted to apologise, but he hadn't given any other reason for wanting to see her again. 'And we would never have had the chance to know each other.'

His voice had changed subtly now. There was the oddest expression in his eyes, and Diana's eyes flickered before them.

'Would that have mattered?' she enquired in a low voice.

'Would it have mattered?' he exclaimed forcefully. 'You have wrought such tremendous changes in my life, Diana, *cara mia*. You have restored my daughter's affection to me. And now Maria is walking, Diana.'

'Och!' She forgot her selfconsciousness before him. 'Och, I'm so glad! I knew . . .'

'*Si*, you knew. And you worked with her towards this happy surprise for me.' He spread his hands in an extravagant gesture. 'How can I show you my gratitude?'

Diana could have told him a way.

'After you left Solamenza, Maria was most distressed. She refused to believe any ill of you.' Wryly, 'She had more sense than her father. When she heard from Faustina that you had gone, and why, she came to me—walking—her vote of confidence in you.'

Diana felt the tears pricking behind her eyes. Again she bowed her head so that he should not see their sheen. She clenched her hands tightly in her lap in an effort to control her turbulent emotions.

'Dear Maria,' she whispered, 'dear wee lassie. And . . . and your aunts and uncles? Do they still think badly of me?'

'In no way!' he said vehemently. 'As soon as I knew the truth, so did they. They are looking forward to welcoming you back to Solamenza.' There was a long intense pause, then he said, 'And so am I.'

There was silence again, a silence that lengthened and grew in intensity. Diana continued to gaze down at her clenched hands, but she could not see them through the blur obscuring her view.

'Diana?' Giacomo said hoarsely. '*Carissima*? You *will* come back to Solamenza? Diana, look at me!'

'I . . . I can't.'

'What do you mean?' His voice was low, hoarse. 'Why can you not come back?'

'I . . . I didn't mean that.'

'Then what, for goodness' sake?' His hands were heavy on her shoulders as though his full weight rested upon her.

'I mean I c-can't look at you,' she said on a hiccuping little sob. 'I don't want you to see what a fool I am.'

A investigative finger beneath her chin tilted up her face and as Giacomo saw her brimming eyes he swore lustily.

'*Madre di Dio*! Have I caused these tears? Have I hurt you again somehow? Diana, *amore mio*,' almost roughly he pulled her into his arms, 'I would not hurt you again for the world. I love you, *carissima*. If you do not agree to come back to me, to be my wife, I shall be the world's most desolate man.'

'Oh, Como!' Through her tears her eyes began to shine. 'You . . . you mean that? You still love me? In spite of . . . ?'

'In spite of nothing!' he said fiercely. 'There is no offence in you. You are good and pure and you have not deserved the unhappiness I caused you. It is I who should doubt that *you* still love *me*.'

'Och, Como!' she said again. Her hands were pressed against his chest, beneath which she could feel the fierce beating of his heart. Her tears spilled over and ran down her cheeks, but now they were happy tears. But at the sight of them he groaned.

'When I think how I have treated you, and when you gave yourself so generously to me. No!' He stopped and fiercely, with all the drama of his Latin blood, said, 'I lie—I *seduced* you. I must be vile in your eyes.'

Diana lifted one hand to press a finger against his lips.

'I won't allow you to denigrate yourself that way,' she told him. 'You had every cause to doubt me. And . . .' she blushed, 'I . . . I'm glad you *did* seduce me—if that's what it was. Though I d-don't remember being very unwilling. Como,' shyly, 'I . . . *do* love you—very, very much.'

With a harsh indrawn breath he crushed her against his chest and she felt his whole body harden.

'Tell me again! Say it again,' he commanded when his grip slackened. 'You cannot say it often enough.'

'I love you.' She stood on tiptoe to breathe the words against his mouth.

'And you will marry me? You will come home to Solamenza?'

'Solamenza! Home!' she said wonderingly. 'Oh, Como, Como! Aye, I'll marry you.'

She felt as if the breath was being squeezed from her body and her pulses beat frantically at his reaction to her words.

'I want you so much, Diana,' he groaned against her hair. 'No man could be your lover once and forget how it was between us.' His words shivered through her, stirring up that familiar excitement in the pit of her stomach. 'It was hell, *cara mia*, sending you away, out of my life.'

'It was hell for me too,' she whispered. 'There hasn't been a night when I haven't remembered what . . . what it was like.'

His hands slid down to her hips, pulling her even harder against him so that she trembled with the violence of his need.

'Oh, Diana!' His voice was thick and then his mouth locked on hers. She could feel the hurried thudding of his heart. He kissed her throat, his fingers tracing the hollows behind her ears, his breathing growing unsteadier.

Diana arched against him, aware of nothing else but a longing to know fulfilment with him again. For a few dizzying moments she felt the full demanding pressure of his thighs. Then he put her from him, leaving her shaking, weak and boneless.

'We shall be married at once,' he said thickly. 'Here in Florence.'

She had no objection to being married as soon as possible. For her it could not be soon enough. But, 'Won't your family be disappointed?' she asked.

'Maybe.' There was desire and anguish in his green eyes. 'But I cannot wait until we return to Solamenza, until Ottavio has been summoned from Rome again. I want you sooner than that, Diana.'

She moved towards him and shyly she set a hand on his arm.

'It would be nice if we could be married at the castle,' she began, and as Giacomo shook his head, 'but that doesn't mean we . . . we have to wait.' She felt the colour rush up into her cheeks as deliberately she opened the floodgates to erotic memories. 'We . . . we didn't wait before.'

His hands cupped her face and he stared deeply into her eyes.

'You would trust me? After what happened last time? Would you rather not wait until we are safely married?'

Though her cheeks were burning at her own temerity, she met his gaze serenely.

'I trust you,' she told him.

'You will let me love you—now?' he said wonderingly.

'Please . . . I want you too,' she told him.

The look in her eyes must have convinced him, for without another word he swung her up into his arms and carried her up the grand staircase of the *palazzo*.

She had not seen this bedroom before, with its carved wood furniture and frescoed panels. But in any case she was not allowed time to study it. Giacomo lowered her on to the bed and bent over her, his lips moving softly, caressingly over hers. She had expected a fierce exorcising of his need, but it was as though he was determined to woo her, determined that they should both extract every ounce of satisfaction from the preliminaries as well as from the final consummation.

His hands began an expert caressing and she reached out for him, seeking for and finding the smooth warmth of his skin beneath his shirt, her fingers in the soft hair that matted his chest. His hands moulded her breasts, his breathing uneven and ragged.

'Last time,' he muttered, 'we were undressed. Undress me, Diana—I want to feel every inch of you against me again.'

As she obeyed he removed her clothes also, with tender expertise, making the removal of each garment part of a worshipping ritual. With every movement her excitement rose and she trembled against him, her lips parting instantly to his kiss.

He was bringing her body to tormenting life, his mouth exploring it with deliberately arousing languor, and Diana gave in blindly to her senses' urging, kissing his neck and shoulders, moaning as he awakened her every nerve until at last his thigh parted hers.

Her passion needed no urging and her body opened to him, inviting his possession, submerging herself in him, giving way to the pulsing need, the hunger. Feverishly her hands caressed his back, her fingertips digging into his flesh as his kiss became almost suffocating in its need. And then he cried out as together their desire exploded into exquisite sensation, followed by the weight of his body heavy on hers.

'Ah, Diana!' As sweet contentment flooded through her he muttered against her neck, 'That was good—so good. And to think how nearly I lost all this! Was it good for you too?' he asked.

'You know it was,' she breathed. She curled against him, her hands moving over his chest, lightly, sensuously, as she breathed in the aroused musky scent of his body.

'And now we must make plans,' he murmured contentedly, 'for our wedding.'

'Now where have I heard that before?' she teased him.

'But this time nothing is going to part us,' he said earnestly. 'The next time we make love we shall be respectably married.'

'Och, I don't know,' Diana said with deliberate provocativeness. As she spoke she traced the familiar paths of his body, her stomach muscles clenching with satisfaction as she felt him jerk convulsively. 'I don't know that too much respectability is a good thing for a descendant of Rainulf Ortoni. There must be *some* of your wicked ancestor's blood in you, surely?'

'If you go on like that,' he growled, 'you'll find out just how much.'

As a warning it failed dismally, and she shook with laughter as she continued her impertinent exploration.

Giacomo turned to look at her, the corners of his mouth curving upwards, and she thought how rarely she had seen him smile. Then he reached out for her.

'To hell with respectability,' said the Eagle of Solamenza.

HARLEQUIN
Romance®

Coming Next Month

#3073 BLUEBIRDS IN THE SPRING Jeanne Allan
After the death of her mother and stepfather, Tracy could have done without a bodyguard—especially Neil Charles. Attractive but arrogant, he clearly held Tracy's wealthy image in contempt. They sparred constantly but she fell in love with him just the same.

#3074 TRUST ME, MY LOVE Sally Heywood
Though it went against her nature, Tamsin had every incentive to deceive Jake Newman on her employer's behalf. Yet when it came to the crunch, she found that Jake's trust in her was the only thing that mattered.

#3075 PLACE FOR THE HEART Catherine Leigh
Florida real-estate developer Felicity Walden knows the Dubois family's Wyoming ranch would make a perfect vacation resort—but Beau Dubois refuses to sell. Still, she's convinced that a cowboy's stubbornness is no match for an Easterner's determination. Even though the cowboy is far too handsome for the Easterner's peace of mind....

#3076 RAINY DAY KISSES Debbie Macomber
Susannah Simmons knows what she wants—career success at any cost. Until she falls in love with Nate Townsend. But her five-year plan doesn't leave room for romance, especially with a man who seems to reject all the values Susannah prizes so highly.

#3077 PASSPORT TO HAPPINESS Jessica Steele
Jayme should have been devastated when she found her fiancé in another woman's arms. But there was no time to brood over the past. She was too busy coping with presently being stranded in Italy in the hands of attractive Nerone Mondadori....

#3078 JESTER'S GIRL Kate Walker
The moment he set foot in her restaurant, Daniel Tyson antagonized Jessica Terry. Though she reacted to him as a stranger, there were two things she didn't know. One was Daniel's unusual occupation; the other was that they'd met—and fought—once before.

Available in September wherever paperback books are sold, or through Harlequin Reader Service:

In the U.S.
901 Fuhrmann Blvd.
P.O. Box 1397
Buffalo, N.Y. 14240-1397

In Canada
P.O. Box 603
Fort Erie, Ontario
L2A 5X3

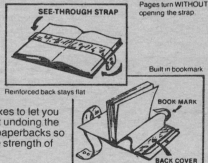

Harlequin Superromance•

THE LIVING WEST

Where men and women must be strong in both body and spirit; where the lessons of the past must be fully absorbed before the present can be understood; where the dramas of everyday lives are played out against a panoramic setting of sun, red earth, mountain and endless sky....

Harlequin Superromance is proud to present this powerful new trilogy by Suzanne Ellison, a veteran Superromance writer who has long possessed a passion for the West. Meet Joe Henderson, whose past haunts him—and his romance with Mandy Larkin; Tess Hamilton, who isn't sure she can make a life with modern-day pioneer Brady Trent, though she loves him desperately; and Clay Gann, who thinks the cultured Roberta Wheeler isn't quite woman enough to make it in the rugged West....

Please join us for HEART OF THE WEST (September 1990), SOUL OF THE WEST (October 1990) and SPIRIT OF THE WEST (November 1990) and see the West come alive!

SR-LW-420-1